EMMA'S
NEW
LOVE

Emma's New Love

The Wish Granters, Book 3

L B Gschwandtner

Cover design by Caroline Murphy
Copy editing by Ross Edwards

Dear Reader:

Let me tell you about two important characters who were introduced in Book One of "The Wish Granters" series: Joe and Alanna. What you need to know about them is this. They're no longer alive. They died in accidents in different places at the very same time. They never knew each other in life but, the thing is, they're not technically dead. They're in what's known as "Transition." And they've been sent back to Earth as a team to grant one wish at a time to one woman at a time. This time that person is Emma.

If you've ever made a wish and hoped it would come true, this story may reassure you that a wish is never in vain. One other thing about Alanna and Joe ... they each have unfinished business of their own back on Earth.

ONE

There Emma was with her boarding pass, a ratty carry-on at her side, and twenty middle-school girls huddled around the chain of plastic chairs waiting for their charter plane to be cleaned and fueled for the trip home.

And there was Mrs. Eddleston engaged in some sort of negotiation at the ticket counter. Yes, Emma called her "Mrs. Eddleston," never by her first name, Maureen, although technically she and Emma were both teachers. Whatever she and the man at the counter were discussing seemed to be going on for much too long and Emma had become impatient to get on with it so they could leave, for pity's sake, which was a phrase her mother used to use. By now it was obvious something was wrong. Definitely wrong.

Oh, God, not the plane, Emma thought. *We can't spend the night in this airport. This is what I hate about charters.*

Not that Emma had taken many charter trips. In fact, this was only the second one with the Willard Girls School Choral Society. The first had been to Toronto. That one lasted only two nights. They'd been in London almost one week now; given three performances; taken in the Tower, Big Ben, and Buckingham Palace; seen the guards change; wandered Piccadilly Circus; gawked inside Madame Tussauds; and eaten enough bangers and mash to last more than one lifetime. And now Emma was impatient to get back to her little apartment and her

1

quiet, solitary life. A week of corralling a gaggle of giggling girls had left her depleted.

Now here was Mrs. Eddleston, turned away from the counter, facing Emma with slightly knitted brows and a frown. She was a solid woman, forty-five-ish with hair dyed an unnatural blond that showed dark roots. In her hand she held what looked unmistakably like a ticket. Emma braced for whatever news was about to be delivered after the few short steps it would take Mrs. Eddleston to traverse the waiting area.

"Well," she began with brows raised, "the good news is that the plane will be ready to board shortly."

Emma raised her own eyebrows in anticipation. And right there, right in that sterile, industrial wasteland of this particular airport lounge, without even thinking consciously about it, Emma's life came into focus. What was her life? What did it consist of?

"I suppose if someone has to stay, you're the logical one," Mrs. Eddleston announced, looking straight at Emma on her return to the waiting area. Was that a note of triumph in her voice? Self-congratulation for sure. A smug little smile. Certainly no regret—no, "so sorry for the inconvenience."

"It's good of you to do this," she added. "Of course you're the logical one," she repeated as if Emma hadn't heard her the first time. "There's no question." Well, that put the point on the pencil.

And there it was. Emma's life in that second of assumption. She was as *expendable* as an appendix. In fact, that was how she often felt: like an appendage. Not part of the pack, not really necessary. A feather blown in on a breeze and just as easily wafted away.

Mrs. Eddleston handed Emma her replacement ticket. "They overbooked. So dumb, but there it is. What can we do?" She gave a disgusted sidelong glance toward the plane waiting outside the big window, but Emma knew that fake smile. It was just like the other times she and the headmistress of Willard Girls School had shuttled off bothersome tasks to her.

If someone had to be stranded in a London airport over Christmas, Emma was the logical one to wait it out alone. She was single and childless, with no one waiting at home for her, no presents under a tree, no tiny lights aglow. Not even parents anymore. A late-life baby, Emma may as well have been raised by grandparents. Her father had died of a stroke while Emma was in college and now her mother, who had no idea where *she* was or who *Emma* was, resided in some forlorn facility supported by years of nursing care insurance premiums her father had steadfastly paid out.

Mrs. Eddleston and the headmistress had used the same argument over the past two years, ever since Emma had taken the job teaching English composition, which consisted mainly of red-penciling papers until they looked as if they'd been through a bloodbath. She'd chaperoned the volleyball team on an overnight bus drive to Hartford, babysat the school mascot (a grossly overweight, incontinent tabby cat), and cleaned up the school van after an attack of food poisoning during a museum trip that ended at a doc-in-the-box outside Providence.

No, she never said it directly, but Emma knew what Mrs. Eddleston meant. You're young, unmarried, the one who can do all the dirty work. The last teacher hired and— if need be—the first one who could be let go if some more

3

agreeable applicant showed her eager face. The threat was never explicitly stated, but ...

Mrs. Eddleston was rounding up the girls now, shooing them like so many chickens into a coop.

This last-minute decision made sense in a way, Emma reasoned in an attempt at fairness, although the whole thing rankled her. They certainly couldn't leave a student on her own in London, and Mrs. Eddleston did have—as she repeatedly reminded Emma—a husband, three children, and a bulldog all anxiously awaiting her return.

Mrs. Eddleston had dragged Emma over to the ticket counter to hear for herself the prospects for leaving London after they were gone. Travel was packed on the twenty-third of December and was even worse on the twenty-fourth. But the harried young ticket agent also had assured Emma that Christmas Day would be better and so would the week after, so she would not only be able to get on a flight, but that she was practically guaranteed a bump to first class.

"Lucky you," Mrs. Eddleston had crowed, and the ticket agent, who shot Emma a surreptitious glance of sympathy with a nod that, without speaking aloud, said yes, first class would be lovely if one didn't mind spending Christmas suspended somewhere between London and Providence, eating airport fare and trying not to focus on how alone you were. Utterly, undeniably, single-girl alone.

The agent then thrust a handful of coupons at Emma. Vouchers for drinks, food, and hotels conveniently located near Gatwick. A massage at the airport spa or a haircut in the salon, whichever she preferred. Most impressively, an extra free ticket to take her anywhere in the world on this particular airline's many routes. So much offered, so little of real value to her.

Where would I go all alone? Emma thought.

She hugged each student goodbye and watched them line up to board their flight. Twenty giddy girls, clutching their bags of souvenirs, wearing sweatshirts from the Globe Theater or the Tower of London, headed home for Christmas and a two-week break from school. Emma maintained a stoic front, but she knew the girls would hiss and gossip about her once they were on the plane. It had been that way ever since Emma herself had been in high school. She felt as if she were still there, not being picked for the cheerleading squad or the softball team. Standing on the sidelines at a dance, hoping to be noticed and at the same time attempting invisibility.

She kept her self-pity hidden, waved with false gaiety until the last of the students had disappeared into the tunnel leading to the plane, and then slumped against a wall. Tears came then in drips down her cheeks. She poked around in her travel purse, the one with lots of pockets, for a tissue to wipe them away, embarrassed at her own fragility, worried that someone might stop, almost hoping someone would. She waited by gate fifty-two. That ticket agent had said someone would bring her bag from the cargo hold. The plane inched back from the jet-way. People still milled about. Strangers. A muddle of jibber jabber, accented English reached her ears. Everything off-kilter. A fish. That's what she was now. A solitary fish in some faraway pond.

After some time, she dragged her carry-on to an empty bank of seats and sat herself down to wait. Soon a bent-over old man showed up rolling her bigger suitcase.

"Is you the lady what's not going on that plane?"

There it was again. One of those odd English accents. She hadn't had time to get used to them yet. At least he wasn't speaking anything totally incomprehensible like Turkish.

"Yes," she answered and stood up, fumbling around in her bag for some leftover pence and came up with two-pound notes.

"Thank you," she handed them over. He blinked and, for a moment, Emma thought maybe she shouldn't have tipped him.

His head bobbed a bit and then he stared at her face.

"Left you, did they? Well no matter," he said. "Pretty girl like you. I tell you what. Go on over to the Bear and Arms down the end of the terminal. Have an ale or stout and order a nice meal for yourself. Ask for Louisa. She'll take good care on ya. Merry Christmas and all."

He tipped an imaginary hat and hobbled off, stuffing the pound notes into a rumpled back pocket. Emma watched him disappear into the milling crowds waiting to board their planes. Everyone seemed to know where they were going. Everyone except her.

What was she going to do in this airport for forty-eight hours? How could she fill this sudden sea of time that now stretched out before her?

And then it occurred to her. *He called me "pretty."*

In fact, Emma *was* pretty. Even sitting there rather worn from this ordeal, she had the kind of cleanly scrubbed face associated with little girls. No makeup and hair that curled naturally over her shoulders, casually pulled away from her face with a rounded velvet strand tied off to one side. It was obvious she didn't fuss over herself. But her blue eyes shone, possibly more than usual from the tears, and they were set rather far apart with sweetly arched brows above them. Nothing in her face seemed out of place. It all fit together with a pleasant (albeit not striking) appearance. There was one thing that set off her looks. Lovely auburn hair, which flowed easily with soft waves and glints of coppery red in sunlight. Her bright, blue eyes were impossible to miss within that frame as they took in everything around her without guile or cunning but with seeming ease. It was only Emma who had not yet discovered her beauty. Sitting there, all she could think about was how to pass this time that had been inflicted on her.

She could use one of these vouchers crammed in her purse to find a hotel. And after that task was complete, she'd be left with, let's see ... approximately forty-seven hours to kill. She could venture down the terminal to the Bear and Arms, probably a dimly-lit pub with a dart board at one end and drunks sloshing pints.

Emma took a deep breath to pull herself together. There was nothing else to do but motor on. The airport was packed with people dragging bags, children running behind them, holiday travelers and families all rushing to their gates.

And then it occurred to Emma: *Okay, this was a shock, but I have to adjust myself to it. Maybe I should look on it as an adventure. I can't be the only person in all of this huge airport stuck and alone.*

Here was an opportunity she so rarely had: to do exactly what she wanted. She should look at this as a gift of time and not squander it by feeling sorry for herself. She had handfuls of vouchers. An airline ticket to anywhere. And no one telling her what to do. No unpleasant tasks and no one she had to watch out for. No one needing her for anything.

Emma looked up and tossed the tissue into a trash bin and then saw, on the schedule board above the gate where she should have left: Next Destination: Edinburgh.

Scotland, she thought. People on that plane will be in Scotland for Christmas. Christmas with soft billowy snow. Tartan plaids, bagpipes, cobblestone streets, little stone bridges over trout streams, strong and dark whiskey, ancient country churches, and sweet little houses with candles in their windows.

And then, as if from a book she'd closed long ago, a page opened. From it came a name in a single breath, like a whisper in her ear. A name she hadn't said to herself or heard in—*how many years was it?*—ten at least. She said it to herself, inaudibly under her breath, and the name evoked the one year when she was happy with herself. The one year—no, that's not right, because it wasn't a whole year but just a few months, a few light-filled months. And now, when the name rested on her lips, she thought, perhaps this was some sort of sign. So she spoke the name out loud.

"Colin MacGregor."

TWO

"So that's really her?" Joe asked Alanna. "The rather forlorn-looking one in the blue sweater?"

"Yes," said Alanna. Squinting at Emma from this distance, it was hard to get a good read.

After receiving their new assignment, the Wish Granters, Joe and Alanna, had manifested, unnoticed, to a corner table at the rear of the room.

Across the Bear and Arms, Emma—now seated at a table where the recommended Louisa, who looked a bit like a bowling ball with hair and squat legs—had led her. She stared into space with a tankard of beer in front of her, the carry-on bag wedged between her feet, and next to her the larger rollaway.

Their file had said she was a teacher at a fancy private school, the sort of ivy-covered place where families sent their daughters as part of a dynastic tradition. But with her long auburn hair and slender frame, this young woman looked scarcely older than a high school student herself.

"Who should go in first?" Joe asked.

Although he and Alanna had worked two cases together before, they were still new to this sort of thing. Even with so little experience they had realized that, at least in the early stages, a woman would feel more at ease talking to another woman. And although their senior coordinator, Morgan, had never explained precisely why, so far she and Joe had only worked with two female clients. Morgan had referred to them as "clients," so Joe and Alanna stuck to that—although Joe thought that was hardly a comprehensive descriptive term for what they were doing. But who was he to argue? Morgan was their boss, their overseer, their all-around go-to guy.

Although it was never explicitly stated, Alanna assumed they'd so far been assigned only women because women have so much trouble wishing for themselves. They know how to wish for their friends, their children, their spouses and boyfriends, and parents. But ask them what they themselves want and women often go silent and timid, often thinking first of what someone else needs or wants, much less taking the steps necessary to realize their own long-abandoned dream. They tuck away their dreams in favor of others, and so those dreams fade like old patchwork quilts, and then fray at the edges and finally crumble from daily disregard.

With a nod to Joe, Alanna said, "I'll go. She looks so lost."

She began making her way through the crowded Bear and Arms. The bustling atmosphere was a good thing, since it gave her a natural excuse to approach Emma, and she knew that the bag she carried—crammed full of brightly wrapped Christmas gifts—would be an effective part of her disguise. The bag was so light that Alanna suspected she was carrying nothing more than empty boxes, but she smiled at Emma as she approached, and asked, "Is this seat taken?"

Emma glanced up from her daydreaming, a bit surprised. She shook her head, and Alanna sat down in the chair opposite her, remembering to drop the bag as if it were truly heavy.

"Thank you," she said. "It's quite a mob, isn't it?"

Emma shrugged, both her hands clasped around her tankard of beer. "Christmas, I guess."

"I guess," Alanna said, signaling to the obviously overworked Louisa, and indicating with a wave of her hand that she'd have the same kind of beer as Emma. Camaraderie could be established over the smallest of things, especially when people were traveling. We're all more unguarded when we're in transit, Alanna thought, and then realized the irony of it all because no one was more in transit than she and Joe. We're all more open and trusting, more likely to confide in strangers. There was an art to drawing the client out. You had to wait for the woman to state her wish, and this could be a delicate task. You could lead her toward it, but she had to say the words all by herself. Until the client states her wish, the Wish Granter can't take the initiative.

"Where are you headed?" Emma asked.

"Scotland," Alanna answered promptly. One of the weird things about being a Wish Granter—one of the thousands of weird things—was that you were given a file on clients before you met them. You could absorb the file in a second and presumably everything you might need to know was contained somewhere within its pages. But the tricky part was that, once you closed the file, the information within was forgotten, at least consciously, and the facts only came back to you in small fragments, arriving just as you needed them. It required a great deal of faith to be a Wish Granter. A willingness to trust in the unknown, to proceed forward on a road, even if you weren't sure exactly where it was leading. Alanna had no idea why she'd just told this pretty young woman in the jeans and blue sweater she was going to Scotland, but she could only assume this was meant to open up further conversation between them.

Emma did flush a little. "Where are you from?" she asked.

Alanna pointed vaguely up toward the ceiling. "It seems like I live in the sky. The name's Alanna, by the way."

Emma took a sip of beer and nodded. "I'm Emma. So you travel for work?"

"Exactly. I travel for work." It was the understatement of all time since Joe and Alanna lived nowhere, belonged nowhere, and were, in fact, in a perpetual state of "on the way to" ...

"Must be exciting."

"Sometimes," Alanna said, leaning back to let the waitress set her own frosty mug in front of her. "But other days I feel I'm never completely here or completely there, you know. I'm like Blanche Dubois, continually depending on the kindness of strangers."

Now why had she said that? Alanna scowled and tried to think of her own past and what was there. It was ironic that she was being sent to help all these women when all she could remember about her own life and death was such a muddle. One thing was sure: When flashes of her life did come back to her, they were shredded bits and pieces of discontent, even rebellion. But against what? There was a lot to learn about this Wish Granter game, and she and Joe were figuring it all out as they went. In the process, they were becoming dependent on each other, which also made Alanna feel a sense of dread on the one hand and comfort on the other. She glanced into the corner and was relieved to see he was still there, playing darts with a couple of men, laughing and slapping them on the back. Joe had an easy, outgoing quality and never seemed to struggle to make friends. It was harder for Alanna, so she turned her concentration back to Emma. She must try harder, she thought.

"Blanche Dubois..." Emma was saying thoughtfully. "It's funny you would mention her. *A Streetcar Named Desire* is my favorite play."

"Mine, too," Alanna said, back on solid ground. Apparently, something about Scotland had been in the file. Something about Scotland and something about Blanche Dubois. She had to learn to trust the process. She often heard herself saying things that didn't make much sense, but her blurted-out statements almost always seemed to draw her closer to the people she'd been sent to help. Had she really liked *A Streetcar Named Desire*? Had she ever even seen the play? It was as if her memory had shattered along with her body on that Florida morning when she'd made the unwise decision to go body surfing alone. It would be simple to say that she'd died that day, but she clearly wasn't dead ... and neither was she exactly alive. The Wish Granters lived in a world between life and death and, while she and Joe had learned that their assigned cases could help move them closer to Heaven or Earth, they hadn't quite grasped how it all worked. Or even which direction they were headed.

"Drama was my favorite class in high school," Emma said, smiling now as she took another sip of her beer. "No one ever knew that. They probably would have guessed I was into chemistry or calculus. I was like the nerd, just one of those brainiacs the other kids make fun of, but somehow junior year I managed to get the lead in the class play. That's why it's so funny you would mention it."

"Ah ... so you're an actress?"

Emma laughed. "Hardly. I teach at a high school in the States. Brought a bunch of students over here on a choral trip and then I was bumped from the flight back."

"So ... you teach drama?"

Emma shook her head. "Not even that. I've tried to get a theater group going back at the school, but our administration doesn't consider the arts a priority. It's our responsibility to get the girls ready for college, produce high SAT scores: measurable proof that their parents didn't waste the megabucks they've paid on tuition. It is most certainly not our jobs to have them singing and dancing their way around the stage." She gave a sad little laugh. "Besides, it's a girls' school. How many times could we do *Sister Act* or *The Women*?"

I don't know what else is going on with this girl, but she's clearly artistically frustrated, Alanna thought. Bored senseless by her job and itching to try something else. She wondered if Emma even knew it.

In the meantime, Alanna smiled too and nodded. Analysis of Emma's personality could wait. The key thing now was to keep her talking. "What play did you do in high school?"

"*Brigadoon*. You know, the old musical." Emma's mouth twisted. "Set in Scotland, by the way, which is ironic considering where you're headed. "

"And you were the lead?"

Emma's face suddenly changed, became infused with joy and a little embarrassment. "Yeah, I was Fiona. The most important male role is Tommy, and he was played by our Scottish exchange student. In fact, that's probably why they chose *Brigadoon* as the class play that year, come to think of it. They knew we had Colin so at least one person would get the Scottish accent right. But then of course

14

they go and cast him as the only American in the play."
Emma giggled. "So here we had twenty American kids
trying to sound Scottish and one Scottish kid trying to
sound American. Crazy."

"Why did they cast Colin as Tommy?"

"Because Tommy is the lead, and Colin can sing and
dance. He was really quite..." she searched for the right
word ... "extraordinary. I don't think I've ever met another
guy quite like him, even after all these years."

Alanna considered the girl. All these years? She'd
guess Emma to be twenty-six at the oldest, but already
speaking wistfully of high school, almost as if that had
been the best part of her life. No one knew better than
Alanna how dangerous it was to become obsessed with
thoughts of the past, how many disappointments lay down
that particular road.

"Memory is a funny thing," Alanna heard herself
saying.

Emma shot her a quizzical look. "Yes," she said. "It
certainly is."

"Would you go back if you could?"

"To high school? Of course not. Who would? I see
how my students suffer over clothes, and gossip and boys
..."

"Especially boys," Alanna said, glancing again at Joe
in the corner, where he was now talking one of his new
buddies into letting him shoot a lemon wedge from his
head with a dart. Alanna could see disaster in the making
over there, but Joe could talk anyone into anything. It was
a quality she envied and, at the same time, resisted.

Emma leaned forward, her face earnest.

She's been crying, Alanna thought. *She's young and
recovers quickly, but when her face is close I can see the redness*

in her eyes, the flush on her cheeks. This poor girl has locked herself into some bathroom stall somewhere in this crowded airport and cried her eyes out.

"If I let you in on something," Emma said, "Will you promise not to tell me that I'm crazy?"

Here it was. Alanna could feel it. The wish. Stated out loud. The moment that would set any number of cosmic forces into motion.

"I promise," Alanna said, bending forward, too.

"I want to find my old boyfriend." Emma sat back and took a deep swig of beer. "If 'boyfriend' is even the proper word. 'Friend' is probably more accurate."

"Colin?"

Emma nodded. "I haven't seen him since we were seniors in high school."

"You said he was a foreign exchange student. Did he live with your family?"

Emma shook her head vigorously. "He was staying at the home of the most popular girl in school. Blonde, cheerleader, rich daddy, expensive car. You know the type?"

"Oh yeah," Alanna said. She suspected that, once upon a time, she might have been that type, but she couldn't get a firm grasp on her own past. It was all like a cloud suspended somewhere far away.

"The kind of girl who's easy to hate," Emma continued. "Or maybe I was just jealous of her. Anyway, he was staying at her house for the year, and he was so cute and had that adorable accent and she treated him ..." Emma paused, took another swig. "She treated him like sort of an exotic pet, you know? Not like a boyfriend or even a brother, but more like the latest thing her parents had bought to amuse her."

16

"But you obviously saw him as boyfriend material."

Emma looked away. "I told you. Colin was different. Special."

"Fiona and Tommy kiss in the play, do they not?"

Emma laughed a bit to cover up her discomfort. "Yes, they certainly do and ... I was only sixteen, you know? Young for a senior. And ... "

"Inexperienced? Was it your first real kiss?"

Emma ignored the question, too busy pulling a handful of papers from her purse. "Look at this. The airline gave me a voucher to go anywhere in the world and there are flights from this airport to Edinburgh six times a day and I have ... I have nowhere to go and at least two days to kill. Longer, if things work out, because the new school term doesn't start until January. It's a sign, don't you think?"

"A sign of what?"

"That I should go to Scotland. When else will I be right here with the money and the time to find out whatever happened to Colin?"

"He's not the only boy you ever ..."

Emma caught her meaning and laughed. "Oh no. God no. There were a couple of guys in college and in fact I just broke up with someone a few months ago. But I always knew it wasn't right. That sounds silly, I guess: a grown women sitting in a bar, talking about some teenaged boy she kissed almost ten years ago and how he meant more to her than anybody since. And this last boyfriend ... I always knew, even from the start ..."

"That you wouldn't end up with him."

Emma nodded vigorously just as a sudden flash of memory made Alanna's gut twist in pain. She hadn't been able to recall much about her time on Earth, but she seemed to have a vague but strong feeling that she, like Emma, had spent years with a man who wasn't The One. Such a ridiculous idea on one level, that, with so many people in the world, fate could swoop down and devise a perfect match. But Alanna sensed she had never fully given up on the notion. Apparently, Emma hadn't either.

Emma lifted her tankard. "I could have ended up with David. He's the kind of man everyone wants you to marry. The kind who looks right on paper. I guess you know that type too?"

"I certainly do," Alanna said fervently.

"But I always knew that David wouldn't be enough for me, not in the long run. So I took this job, moved to Providence, and made myself a promise. That Colin is the standard. I won't end up with any guy unless it feels as right with him as it did with Colin that night backstage, behind the curtains, when he kissed me."

"Behind the curtains? I would have guessed that Fiona and Tommy kissed on stage."

Emma giggled. "He said we needed to practice."

Alanna leaned in again, dropped her voice. "Tell me the truth. You said you wanted to see Colin again, just to know what happened to him. But people don't fly from one country to another out of idle curiosity. You'd pick up the phone or try to find him on the Internet. What are you really wishing for? Another kiss?" If Emma knew who and what Alanna was, she would have known this was a ruse to get the wish stated out loud. Because without that, Alanna was powerless to grant it.

"Or maybe just to know if that kiss was real." Emma's face grew a little more pensive. "Here's the thing. When David and I broke up last year, I told myself I needed to find a guy like Colin, and it's just in the last hour that I

18

realized I could actually find Colin himself. Remember what I felt. See if he's still the same person. See if I'm the same person too, I guess." She gave a rueful chuckle. "You must think I'm very silly."

"I wouldn't say 'silly.'" Alanna looked back in the corner where Joe was now choosing teams for a dart game challenge. Yeah, he could be an overgrown frat boy, especially when he was bored, but this would be a swell time for him to appear. She'd like to get his unsentimental masculine take on the situation. Emma hadn't yet stated her wish clearly enough, but it seemed to Alanna like a very emotionally dangerous enterprise. It had been ten years since Emma had even seen this Colin boy. Who knew where he was now, how his life had turned out, or if he even remembered the shy, bookish girl he'd kissed in a high school play? And what could Alanna and Joe do to move this into the romance sphere if they did meet up again? Alanna wondered about the limitations of their own powers. It didn't end with the wish, but how far could they interfere?

"I wouldn't say 'silly,'" Alanna repeated slowly. Morgan had told them several times that, crazy as it may seem, it was never their job to talk a client out of a wish. "But it seems like you're making a pretty big assumption that he'll still be in Edinburgh. There's no way to let him know you're coming?"

Emma shook her head with a small giggle. "Colin lived in this tiny little town named Alloway just out from a town named Ayr, which is pretty far from Edinburgh. He used to call it 'a wee village.' Isn't that adorable?"

"Adorable," Alanna said dryly, trying to signal to Joe with her eyes. "Maybe you could fly to somewhere closer."

Emma shook her head. "I put myself on standby for every flight to Edinburgh and they said they'd text me on my cell if a seat opened up on one. I know it's not very likely, it being right before Christmas and all, but if someone somewhere misses a connection ..." She sat back, a look of resignation on her face. And then, out of nowhere, she said it.

"I wish I could see Colin just once. Just to satisfy myself one way or the other and either move forward with my life or let it go. But the planes are so full and there's so little time."

"I have a feeling a seat will open up," Alanna said.

"Really?"

Emma's face brightened with hope, and she smiled at Alanna, who returned the smile. Now that the wish had been stated, Alanna and Joe could get to work on making it happen. Not that she didn't still harbor doubts. Of course, Joe would be all over this. It was one of the qualities Alanna had come to depend on: that Joe never hesitated. He just assumed whatever he decided was right and went ahead to make it happen.

"Call it a hunch. And lately my hunches are quite reliable."

Oh really? She thought. *We're only going to fly to Scotland on a whim to find this MacGregor guy is married and has a cute little cottage full of screaming brats and a bedraggled fishwife, old before her time, dressed in second-hand clothes and whining about money. Or maybe Colin won't even be there but rather down at the local pub, a fat slobbery drunk begging for his next pint and betting on some fistfight out back. Poor Emma. What a letdown that would be.*

Alanna hesitated. Maybe this was one wish that shouldn't be granted. But hadn't Morgan told them, that

20

first time in Transition when she and Joe were so new at this, unschooled and completely bewildered, that it wasn't their job to edit a client's wish. They were not to pick and choose but to grant the wish and let it go where it would. Just keep a steady eye on the progress and try to help where possible. That was their only mandate. So she figured it would probably do Emma good just to have her curiosity satisfied. Besides, Alanna had no reason to be such a naysayer. Every woman likely had an old boyfriend who still occupied a protected spot in her adult heart. Who wouldn't want one more moment with the one who got away? Even if it was just to be reassured that getting away was, in the end, the right thing to happen. Emma's wish may have been untenable on one level yet understandable on another.

"You never told me where you're going," Emma said.

"It's the most amazing coincidence," Alanna said, turning back toward Emma. "But I'm spending Christmas in Edinburgh, too."

THREE

Joe had drained his beer and now plunked the glass down on the worn wooden table. Still holding the handle, he swiveled his head to look straight at Alanna as if challenging her decision to grant this wish. "I'd like to go on record right now that this was a stupid idea."

"Are you saying she shouldn't wish for what she wants?" Alanna asked. She stared out the frosted window into the snowy street outside. Flakes drifted down from the night sky, everything muffled and quiet. It was a cushiony kind of snow, not some blustery storm. Still and cold, but somehow comforting. Alanna had a vague feeling of unfamiliarity and wondered about its origin. There was so much she no longer knew. She wondered, also, if Joe felt the same kind of floating that sometimes enveloped her. Well, maybe it was normal. After all, this being in Transition was supposed to feel rootless.

"It's not what I would wish for," Joe was back at that wish. "I'll bet you it's not going to get her anything."

"How do you know what she wants it to get her? Maybe she just wants to see what path she should take now. Not everything is a zero-sum game, you know."

"Of course it is. Take this situation. If she finds this MacGregor character, he's either going to be the love she lost or an SOB she doesn't want anymore. Either way she's lost something. And naturally, when someone loses something, someone else gains."

"You've just watched too much football and played too many hands of poker." Alanna looked away from the window. "Anyway, if we don't step in, she's not going to get the chance at her zero-sum, because that cab isn't going to take her anywhere tonight." She pointed outside and Joe looked out the window.

She and Joe had been able to manifest from the airport bar straight into this dark pub. Morgan had been right when he'd told them they could appear and disappear with no effort. Poor Emma: At the last minute, a seat had opened up on a bumpy prop-plane flight into Edinburgh. Even worse, she was now standing out on the snow-covered curb wearing wholly inappropriate foot gear for this weather, negotiating with a local man to drive her to Alloway, the wee village Colin MacGregor had once called home. The conversation evidently was not going well. The man must be demanding a steep fee to transport her sixty kilometers through the Scottish Highlands, not to mention it was after ten o'clock on Christmas Eve and the weather seemed to be getting worse by the minute. Joe and Alanna watched as Emma made increasingly pleading hand gestures, finally opening her wallet up as far as it would go to show the man she really didn't have any more money.

"She's going all in on this," Joe said. "Especially considering she doesn't even know if the guy is still around. What happens if she gets there at midnight in a snowstorm and can't even find him? Does this little burg even have a hotel?"

"I don't know," Alanna said warily. "And even if it does, it's Christmas Eve, and she's showing up out of the blue with no reservations. We could all be heading toward one of those 'no room at the inn' situations. She might end up sleeping in a barn wrapped in hay."

Joe slowly shook his head. "I've got a bad feeling about this whole thing."

"Which I believe you've already said. But if Morgan was here, he'd tell us ..."

"That it isn't your job to tell a woman what to wish for," came a deep, familiar voice.

Morgan slid into the booth beside Joe. "If you think you two have problems," he said. "How would you like to be me, an aging black man trying to keep a low profile in Scotland?"

Joe laughed and signaled the barmaid for another beer. When he and Alanna had first met their senior coordinator up in Transition, they hadn't known what to call him. He didn't like the word "boss," and he sure didn't like the word "God." He said that particular term of address always seemed to make people either awestruck or terrified. So instead they'd settled on Morgan, a nickname based on the man's uncanny resemblance to the actor Morgan Freeman. But whatever he was, it was a relief to see him in Edinburgh. Each time Joe and Alanna got stuck, Morgan seemed to know how to get the situation rolling again.

"Your young lady is headed to a very lovely place," Morgan said, going into the sing-song voice of a tour guide. "Alloway is one of the most picturesque villages in Scotland, birthplace to the poet Robert Burns, and home to a particularly quaint bridge over the river Doon."

"Bridge over the river Doon?" Alanna asked sharply. "As in *Brigadoon*?"

Morgan nodded. "Very good. Go to the head of the class."

24

"Okay, you two are going to have to slow down for us special needs kids," Joe said. "What the hell is a Brigadoon?"

"It's a play set in Scotland," Alanna said. "Evidently set in Alloway itself. They made one of the old MGM musicals about it. You know, lots of singing and dancing and guys leaping around in kilts."

Joe frowned. "I've always been more of the action film type. Clint Eastwood, Star Wars, Batman."

"Imagine my surprise," Alanna said coolly. "Anyway, more to the point of our particular situation, that's the play Emma and Colin were in together as teenagers. He was a Scottish exchange student, so they chose not just a Scottish play, but one that was set in his very own hometown. They played the lead roles and he kissed her, and now she's on a quest to recapture that feeling."

"He kissed her?" Joe said skeptically. "That's all?"

"Men," Alanna shook her head in dismay. "A kiss is the beginning of everything. It can mean much more than the other stuff, if you want to know the truth."

"Well, if that's the case, the man she's infatuated with must not know much about the other stuff," Joe said. "If it were me ..."

"But it isn't you," Alanna said. "And I don't think we should be talking like this in front of Morgan."

Morgan shrugged. "I've heard worse."

"So does this play have a plot?" Joe said. "Between the dancing and singing and leaping and kissing, I mean?"

"Very good question," Morgan said amicably. "Really, the two of you are catching on quite fast. The play is about two American men who stumble onto a small, mythical town in Scotland that only comes alive for one night every one hundred years, and, needless to say, they just happen to arrive on the magic night. One of the men, Tommy, falls in love with a lassie from the village. But if anyone leaves Brigadoon, the magic spell will be broken and the village will cease to exist."

"She can't come with him, so he has to decide whether or not to stay with her in a world that isn't really real," Joe says. "See, this is exactly why I don't watch chick flicks. They always put people in these impossible situations, stuck between two worlds. They don't make any sense."

"Listen to who's talking about being stuck between worlds," Alanna pointed at Joe.

"Okay," he said. "So it's not exactly a logical position for me to take at this particular time."

"But it makes perfect sense," said Alanna. "It's just another variation on Romeo and Juliet. The lovers who can't be together. Star crossed. But what does the plot of the play have to do with Emma? She isn't going out in the snow looking for a town that doesn't exist, is she?"

"Oh no, Alloway is real enough," said Morgan. "At least for now. But they take in months worth of profit in a single night on New Year's Eve, when they stage an annual rendition of *Brigadoon* in the very town that inspired the play. People travel from as far away as London to see it. Quite the tradition and quite the little moneymaker. Without it, Alloway ..."

"Might cease to exist," Joe finished for him. "Terrific. The play is about a town that disappears and, without the play, the town might really disappear—or at least go belly up."

"And Emma's showing up a week before the annual performance," Alanna said, peering anxiously out the window to the street, where the driver had thrown up his

26

hands in exasperation and was walking away from Emma. The girl's shoulders slumped in discouragement and snow was starting to pile up on the brim of her hat. "Showing up just as they're restaging the show where Colin kissed her."

"Does she really just want to find him?" Joe said, skeptically. "It seems to me she's claiming to wish for one thing—which is just to know what happened to her old buddy Colin. But my bet is that she really wants something else. Like for him to fall in love with her. Or for them to be like, poof, magically fifteen again. My guess is that she didn't fly all the way out here to MacHootersville just looking for a little lip lock. If you ask me ..."

"Maybe you don't know as much about women as you claim. Trust me. A kiss can mean everything on Earth to a woman," Alanna whispered.

Joe stared at her as if seeing Alanna for the first time. He was about to take up this challenge when Morgan spoke.

"That leads me to the final thing I need to tell you. On the last case, the two of you came to depend on each other quite a lot. Which is to be expected and which is really quite appropriate for a team of Wish Granters ... up to a point."

Alanna tensed from head to toe. Where was this heading? She could sense Joe still looking at her and she didn't want to betray her feelings.

"But we don't want you two distracted," Morgan went on. Alanna turned away, a sudden flush turning her cheeks hot. He was saying that he knew Joe had kissed her back on their last assignment, that he was aware some spark had ignited between them. But of course he knew. Morgan knew everything.

Joe was also uncomfortable, even though his years as a lawyer in an Earthly courtroom had made him better at both hiding his emotions and changing the subject. It was this training and experience that kicked in now, even if he didn't precisely remember it. Still, it was there.

"Why would we be distracted?" he asked. "You've made it clear enough what you expect of us. What you haven't made clear is what we get in return. Okay, so we swoop in and help these women. We give them what they say they want, even if we don't think their wish has any real value. And each time, what? We're earning points we cash in at some later date? We're getting one more step closer to our own lives back on Earth? Because I've told you before I have plenty of unfinished business that I need ..."

"We won't get distracted," Alanna broke in. She knew it was pointless for Joe to rant in front of Morgan, who had been completely unmoved by all of Joe's previous arguments. Joe seemed to argue by instinct, and had trouble holding his tongue if there seemed to be even the slightest chance he might get his way.

Besides, Morgan had a point. Their focus should be on their cases, not on their burgeoning attraction to each other. Falling into each other's arms like they'd done back there at another time may have been a mere momentary impulse. They'd both just been through horrible accidents, which had ripped them abruptly from their Earthly lives. They were hovering somewhere between life and death, in a world called Transition that seemed to have many layers and many rules. Then Morgan had shown up and told them they were going to be something called Wish Granters, a job they didn't understand at all back then. A job they were still struggling to understand.

Of course they had turned to each other. Of course they had reached out for the only understandable and comforting thing in this crazy new world, but Alanna also knew that loneliness and desperation, no matter how understandable under the circumstances, were no basis for a love affair. Joe had made it very clear he wanted to return to Earth and all that unfinished business he'd left behind, while she ...

Well, Alanna wasn't entirely sure yet what she wanted, but she suspected that she and Joe were headed in opposite directions. For whatever reason, Morgan and the other powers above had partnered them as Wish Granters. But that didn't mean the partnership was permanent. And, dead or alive, one thing was sure: She wasn't going to keep getting involved with guys unless she knew there was a future in it. Trouble was, she couldn't quite remember what had gone wrong back there in her other life on Earth. She had captured bits and pieces, but the whole puzzle had not yet been reassembled and, until she could put the picture together, there was no reason to get involved in something new.

"Granting Emma's wish is our top priority," Alanna said firmly. "In fact, it's our only priority."

Joe nodded, but Alanna noticed he had been ripping his bar napkin into neat little strips during this last part of the conversation, his fingers tediously making sure that each piece was uniform and even. That was one of the things that Alanna found attractive in Joe. He was tenacious and precise.

"Yeah, yeah, we're all business," he said. "And expecting that a successful conclusion to this case will take us another step closer to where we want to go. Right?"

"Thank you both for being so understanding," Morgan said. He drained his beer, ignored Joe's last try at getting the information he wanted, and fished a plaid cabbie hat out of his pocket, slid it onto his head and pulled it down low across his forehead. "Now you'll have to excuse me. It would appear I have a fare waiting in the snow."

"What? You mean you're going to drive her cab?" Joe raised his voice so that Alanna looked around to see if anyone noticed.

"Shh," she said and turned to Morgan, eyebrows raised with the same question.

"Why? Don't you think I'm a good driver?"

"Well, sure, but you said yourself it's hard to keep a low profile for you. I mean, honestly, you can't exactly pass yourself off as some Scottish cabbie."

"You just watch me, sonny."

With that he stood up and left the pub.

FOUR

As the car slowed down in front of a small church, the cabbie asked, "Are you sure this is the place, Miss?"

Emma wasn't sure of anything, especially who her cab driver was. It was late and the entire town appeared to be asleep. Dark and silent, with the snow turning everything into soft mounds of white. They had crept their way along the winding road from Edinburgh for over an hour, finally inching across the ancient, small stone bridge and into Alloway to find only a single building lighted. This church.

"Whole village at a midnight church service would be my guess, Miss," the cabbie added, when it became clear Emma had nothing say.

Of course. A midnight service on Christmas Eve at a church which looked like it had come alive from a postcard. Incredibly quaint and at the same time frightening. Here she was. And where was that? Would she be regarded as some odd interloper, a wayward tourist who had no business in their little town?

"I suppose the village church is as good a place to start as any," Emma said shakily, reaching for her bag. She handed him the agreed-upon number of pounds, wondering again why he'd been so much cheaper than the first driver she'd tried to book. When he'd first appeared back in Edinburgh and seemed so eager to drive her to this out-of-the-way location late on Christmas Eve, Emma had been a little uneasy. She wasn't falling into the hands of some criminal cabbie, was she? But he told her they had something in common—Americans in Scotland at Christmas—and he said he was there working on research for a book and driving a cab gave him a chance to make a little money at the same time he was getting to see the countryside. He especially liked fares that took him out of the city. So he'd taken her straight to Alloway, without fuss, navigating the icy country roads like an expert and making even better time than promised.

Pulling her suitcase with the carry-on stacked on top behind her, Emma left the cab and her foot immediately sank into a pile of snow. At that moment she was keenly aware of her inadequate shoes, so she struggled to drag the bag to the shoveled sidewalk and up the three small steps when it suddenly occurred to her that she should have asked the driver to wait. What if she was unable to find Colin—or any place at all to stay?

But when she turned, the cab was gone.

Now, that was strange.

Very strange. It had been slow driving across the bridge and into town coming in, so how could he be out of sight so quickly?

Either way, here she was. The end of the trail. Or perhaps the beginning of a new trail. Whether she found Colin or not, she'd be spending Christmas in Alloway.

Emma pushed open the door and stepped into a vestry that was nearly as cold as the street. Stamping her feet and shaking the snow off her hat and muffler, she pushed her suitcase against the wall and paused at the sound of a carol coming from the chapel. "Silent Night." Corny maybe, but somehow soothing. Certainly appropriate, and the sweet voices of children among the singers caused Emma to stop and listen.

As they sang the last chorus with its final verse about heavenly peace, Emma slipped quietly into the sanctuary. It took a moment for her eyes to adjust to the candlelight. The church was neither what she'd imagined nor as old as she'd thought it would be. It seemed her fantasy of where Colin lived was just that: an imagining. Maybe this whole idea was nothing but a childish whim. But the stone church was lovely, larger than she'd imagined, and grander—with enough pews that she felt intimidated, as all the pews seemed crammed full of worshippers. As she stood there assessing her options, the minister in the pulpit, who was the only person facing in her direction, noted her arrival. While the parishioners settled down in their seats after the caroling, they adjusted their coats and hymnbooks and shushed children. Someone coughed and the minister, an older man with a shock of white hair around a pink-cheeked face, looked straight at Emma and, with a wave of his hand, indicated a small gap in one of the pews down near the front.

Too late to turn back now, Emma realized, and she made her way as inconspicuously as possible down the aisle and worked her way into the pew. She squeezed in beside a motherly-looking woman whose peppered, gray hair was pulled into a low bun. When the woman smiled at her and made as much room as she could, Emma suddenly felt welcomed and not quite so out of place.

As she wedged her way into the seat, it struck Emma that it really was the way she'd always pictured it: the approach across the bridge, the river Doon, the shops, the snow-covered yews, and, when she was able to really see the whole town in the light of day, perhaps it wouldn't be such a stretch to have come here. She could easily pass herself off as a tourist, a lover of poetry, just one of those

Americans who came to see where Robert Burns had lived and composed his verses. Her feet were cold, the melted snow having reached inside. Still seated under the high arches of the ceiling above, she felt peaceful for the first time since she'd left for London with the girls and Mrs. Eddleston. They were already becoming a memory of the past she'd stuffed away, and her present seemed, at least for the moment, hopeful that she'd made the right decision. Whatever had happened to Colin MacGregor was a matter only time would reveal.

As the minister took up the service, for Emma, right now, it was as if time hovered somewhere beyond her reach. And yet she knew time had moved on and so had she. But not in everything, not in some little place in her heart where she'd hidden that moment, that kiss, that first real thrill of love.

The minister read from the gospels and Emma began to look around. She tried to be as unobtrusive as possible, but who was she kidding? She was the proverbial sore thumb in this little holiday scene. The late arrival of a total stranger at the service was already causing a stir among the congregation. When Emma glanced over her shoulder, she found dozens of pairs of eyes fixed straight on her. The elderly organist was gaping at her so openly that it took quite a bit of throat-clearing from the minister to snap the woman from her reverie and signal it was time to start the music for communion.

The minister lifted a cloth from the altar to reveal a silver cup so worn and battered that, as far as Emma was concerned, it might well have been the original Holy Grail. Beside it was a long brown loaf of clearly homemade bread and, as he began the familiar words of the ceremony, Emma relaxed a little. She hadn't seen

Colin yet, but that didn't mean he wasn't here. Or that, even if he wasn't at this particular church service, someone in this town wouldn't know how to find him. It looked as if the entire citizenry of Alloway was crammed into these pews. So he should be there.

The words of the communion service came to a close. Two men stepped forward to help the minister pass the wine and bread. One was an older man with a farmer's weathered face, but the other ...

Emma squinted in dim light afforded only by many candles. Was this the Colin she'd pictured so many times—the Colin she'd romanticized so fully? He had the same dark hair and thick eyebrows. She wasn't sure about his age, but he seemed to fit the time that had elapsed. But there was something off, not exactly the same. Well, of course years had gone by. He would have changed, surely. But how much and in what ways? Could her memory of Colin have become like Brigadoon itself—alive for a fleeting moment and then, poof, no longer really there? No matter how hard she stared at the man in front of her now, willing him to look up and meet her eyes, he remained focused only on the silver cup before him.

It was the sort of church where the congregation approaches the altar, row after row, like a high school graduation ceremony. Emma waited with some anxiety for her turn and then followed the woman with the low bun to the front of the church. She bowed her head in front of the farmer and let him place a bit of the rough bread on her tongue. Bowed again before the minister, who gently chanted the words of the sacrament. And came finally to the younger man on the end, the one with the wine, the one who could be Colin. She played a little game in her head, like a child's game. If he looks up and smiles, then he recognizes me and it is Colin. If he doesn't smile, then it can't be him.

Emma kept her head lowered, watched his hands extend the silver cup. Had these hands ever reached for hers, ever lifted her chin for a kiss? She closed her lips around the rim of the chalice and then her teeth clinked against the silver, which gave her a little jolt before the wine sloshed into her mouth. She took in more than she'd intended and, for one brief moment, she imagined it coming back out, splattering all over, and there she would be: a post-adolescent stranger mooning over some supposed lost love in a town that had not invited her and where she did not belong. The moment passed, the wine slid down her throat, and she cautiously lifted her gaze.

He stared right at her. No smile. Not even a hint of recognition.

It was too much to contemplate in the moment and she stood, a bit shakily. The man before her was not as tall as she remembered, standing as they were now, so close to each other. She'd had to lean far back and tilt her face up toward Colin for their kiss. He was certainly taller than this. And this man was striking in a different way. Not the way Colin was handsome, not that self-assured teasing way about Colin. But people change, she reminded herself. They can lose a lot of self confidence when life treats them harshly. Could that have happened to him? No, she thought: He would still have that glint in his eye. And this young man seemed poised at the edge of something, as if he was about to spring into action. And his eyes, when they met hers for an instant, seemed to burn right through her, like he knew what she was thinking, knew why she had come here, knew her better than she knew herself. No, she had to gain control of her emotions, but she couldn't stop the blush from creeping up her neck and across her cheeks.

Enough. She was in a church, on Christmas Eve, taking communion. And she was being a fool. This man wasn't Colin; he was merely a shorter, stockier version, and if she'd kept her wits about her she would have seen that half the people in the pews had this same dark heavy-browed look. This man was probably some distant cousin, maybe even a brother. But he was not the one she had traveled so far to see.

The church bells began to chime. Just overhead and so loud that the whole room seemed to vibrate and shimmer with the sound. One. Two. Three. Four. Five. The man was staring at her. Emma stared back. Six. Seven. Eight. He opened his mouth as if to speak. Nine. Ten. Eleven. She gave him a tentative smile. Twelve.

It was midnight. It was Christmas.

"Peace be with you," the man said.

"And also with you," Emma said automatically, turning back to her seat.

The mood within the church had shifted slightly with the ringing of the midnight bells. The reverence of the Eve had given way to the gaiety of Christmas Day. Everyone stood to sing "Joy to the World," then some carol that Emma had never heard, and then the candles were blown out, the lights came on overhead, and everyone turned to gather their things.

They were all chattering, visiting among themselves. Emma decided the minister was as likely a place to begin as any, and she moved up the aisle.

"Welcome, my dear," the man said, with a slight rolling of the "r." He held out a hand to her. "We're so glad you could be with us on this holy night." His hand was warm and dry. His smile so open that whatever nervous reserve Emma still harbored fluttered away like a falling leaf.

"I am too," she said, and realized how very true that was. Even if she never did find Colin, this was a most beautiful Christmas Eve—one that she would treasure.

"I'm a visitor here," she went on, an obvious statement but by way of introduction it seemed appropriate enough. The minister watched her with a kindly, expectant expression.

"Oh, yes," he said. "We get so many people here for the big show. You've arrived a bit early, but no matter. We're always happy to see new faces, especially inside this church. Or," he went on, "perhaps you've come to visit the Robert Burns house and museum. I'm afraid the garden's lying fallow at the moment."

His burr had emerged in all its Scottish fullness, and Emma found it and his manner disarming enough that she was emboldened to ask, "Would you happen to know a young man named Colin MacGregor?"

"Ah," the minister said, as if this explained everything. "So you're not one of our regular visitors to the sites of Alloway." And he continued, "Yes, Colin. Of course I know him, and it was his Aunt Aileen you were seated beside. Come this way." She followed him toward a huddle of women chatting in the back of the sanctuary.

"I'm the Reverend Dunn," he said as they walked. "And I baptized Colin as a boy. Most of the people in this church, in fact. I guess that makes me very old indeed." He chuckled at himself and again, Emma found this disarming, as if she had known him for years. "And what would be your name, if I may ask?"

"Oh, I am sorry. Emma. That is Emma Riordan."

"So you have some Irish in you? We're practically cousins, then."

Again he chuckled. They were approaching the women, who all turned as one to greet her. A new face in town and they were about to find out why.

"I bring you ladies the fair Emma Riordan," Dunn said. "Who has come here all the way from America, it seems, seeking Colin MacGregor."

"From America, it is then," said Colin's Aunt Aileen. "All that way, lass?"

"Well," she began, not quite sure how much to explain on the spot. "Sort of. It's a long story."

"Well, isn't this a Christmas miracle?" Aunt Aileen said. "I must say, Colin has spoken of you often, of his time in the States. When Colin was an exchange student, they presented *Brigadoon* in his honor," she added, turning by way of explanation to the other ladies in the circle, who were clearly curious. "And Emma was in the theater troupe as well, weren't you, lass?"

"I was Fiona and Colin was Tommy," Emma said.

"Well of course he was," Dunn said with a chuckle. "Colin is always Tommy. Has played the part in our little village musical ... how many years is coming up on, ladies? Nine? Ten? And will play it again, come next week, on New Year's Eve, just as he always has."

"Oh, then he's still here," Emma said. "I mean in Alloway." There was relief mixed with something else in her voice—apprehension perhaps. If he was still there, then she would definitely see him again. And then what? Sometimes the thought, or the hope of something in the future turns into disappointment and regret when it happens. For Emma, this spur-of-the-moment trip into the past was, in reality, not going back at all. She could see that now. And then ...

"Of course he's here, my dear," said Aunt Aileen. "No one ever really leaves Alloway, although Colin keeps trying, poor lad. Well, actually, I should say he still lives here, although he's not in town for the moment."

"We're not being very clear, are we?" said a young woman. She was blonde, pretty, sweet-faced, closer to Emma's age, and Emma turned to her with relief. Perhaps she would actually explain things in some reasonable fashion. "My name is Skye, by the way, and what his aunt Aileen is trying to explain is that Colin has gone to London for Christmas."

"Not by choice," Aunt Aileen added. Her mouth set hard as she spoke, as if a trip to London was something that tasted bad, like a bitter fruit.

So he had been in London when Emma was there. She might have passed him on a street, have stood in the same line at the airport, or ordered food in the same café. But she would have seen him. Surely she would recognize him. But would he know her? It had been so long. And what was one kiss, after all?

"Colin's wife, or perhaps I should say ex-wife, or perhaps I should say soon-to-be ex-wife ... anyway, she's from London," Skye said. "Village life never quite suited her, did it? So she went back to the city and took their little daughter with her. If Colin is to spend Christmas with his child, he must do it in London, and so that's where he is."

"He'll be back for New Year's of course," Aunt Aileen said. "For the play."

"Colin wouldn't miss the play," a woman in the group murmured.

40

"Not the play," said another.

They all nodded in unison as if they'd all read the same instruction from a play. *Everyone nods here.*

"Yes," said Dunn. "As he's our Tommy every year, as I mentioned, and Skye has taken the part of Fiona for—how many seasons is it now? Oh yes, five."

"I smell problems," Joe said. He and Alanna had watched the action from up in the choir loft.

"This town is wonderful," Alanna said. "The snow, the stone buildings, that little arched bridge with snow-covered ivy. The Robert Burns cottage. Like a fairy tale."

"It's all right, I guess. If you like that sort of thing. I got over small old towns a long time ago, being from New England, where you can't spit without hitting another Ye Olde Inne."

"You can't be that immune to the charm of it all," she said. "A tiny gem of a place. And these people ..."

"These people are part of the complication," Joe said. "Haven't you been listening at all? Colin's not even divorced yet and he's already got a new girl."

"Colin's already got a co-star," Alanna said. "That's not the same thing as having a girl. You heard them. He's getting divorced, he'll soon be available, and apparently he's a good father to his little girl in London. Everything is coming together just fine."

"You'll stay for the play, won't you?" Aunt Aileen was saying below, as she reached out to pat Emma's arm. "After all, you've come all this way to see Colin ..."

41

"I wasn't planning to stay until New Year's," Emma said. "I'm a teacher..."

"Out for the Christmas term, I presume," said Dunn. "Then Aileen is right, just as she always is. You must stay with us through the New Year and see Colin in *Brigadoon*."

"If you could show me to a hotel..."

The circle burst into laughter, as if Emma had requested a hot air balloon or a perhaps a lunar module.

"With the New Year's play, our whole little village becomes a hotel, you might say," Skye explained. You see, everyone in town rents out their spare rooms during the New Year's festival. It's a wonderful tradition and brings in so much more than anything else during these dark winter months."

"People come from everywhere for our little theatrical offering," Dunn said proudly. Edinburgh. Aberdeen. London ..."

"Even America, it would seem," said Aunt Aileen. "You'll stay with us, Emma. Colin's room is empty, and he'll be so pleased and delighted to return from London and find you here ..."

"What did I tell you? A complication," Joe said. He peered over the balcony to get a better view of the circle of women and Reverend Dunn.

"Shhh ..." Alanna said.

"They can't hear me."

"Maybe not, but why take the chance? This is all working out perfectly."

"How do you figure that? Yeah, we've got her in his bed, but he isn't in it. He isn't even in the country."

Alanna sighed. "He's coming back, isn't he?"

"I couldn't possibly impose on you like that," Emma said, although, if she'd been honest with them or herself, she would have admitted a little thrill ran through her at Aunt Aileen's offer. The idea of staying with Colin's aunt, of sleeping in his very room, was more than she could have hoped for. Granted, he hadn't been waiting here in the village like she'd dreamed, he hadn't run across the little bridge in the snow to embrace her, but this was almost as good. He'd be back within days and she'd be waiting.

"Nonsense, Aileen's house is the perfect place for you," said Dunn, as if it all were settled. "Do you have a bag, my dear?"

"I left my suitcase in the vestry," said Emma and smiled at him.

"I'll get my son to carry it," said Aileen. "Brodie? Come here, dear; we've found ourselves a boarder a few days early."

The young man who'd served the wine turned from his own group of friends toward his mother. His eyes locked on Emma's with such intensity that she turned away. It was the same feeling she'd had before but she couldn't figure out exactly what that feeling was. Or maybe it wasn't one feeling but a tangle of interlocking sensations, like being at an amusement park and riding all the rides at one time. There was exhilaration and a bit of

fear. There was excitement and a moment of caution.
There was an overriding feeling of being lifted
momentarily off her feet and yet her feet, still damp inside
her shoes, were certainly solidly on the church floor.

"This is my son, Brodie," Aileen said. "Colin's
cousin, of course. And he'll drive us straight home, won't
you dear?"

"And another shoe falls," Joe said.

Alanna said, "I think you're just looking for trouble.
What will you do if she doesn't even need anything else
from us?"

"In that case, we'll just have to make the best of a bad
situation," Joe answered and reached for her arm.

"Joe," she whispered, "you know what Morgan told
us back at the airport. We can't. You have to watch out."

"What can he do to us anyway? We're already not
alive."

"I don't have any idea, but I think there must be
worse places we could be."

"Don't tell me you believe in some Hell where fires
will burn us for eternity if we just have ..."

"Joe," she pulled away. "I do believe in some things. I
do believe that we have to do what Morgan says. And I do
believe you're going to get us into big trouble if you don't
control your urges."

"Tell me, then. Do you believe in Hell?"

"I don't know. I never did, but now I'm not at all
sure what I believe. I never would have believed this." She

44

made a motion with both hands that clearly took in the two of them and their situation.

"Well, I do not. Definitely not. But the next time we see Morgan I plan to get an explanation about it. And as for urges, you weren't exactly reluctant on our last job down here."

"I know, and I regret that."

"Oh, really? I'm sorry to hear you say it. I never had any complaints before. Of course, we did get pulled back up—or wherever it is they pull us when they take us out of here—before anything really happened. I mean anything much."

Joe sighed and looked as if he'd lost a puppy. It was in such moments that Alanna's feelings for Joe really emerged. He could be such a guy—all brash and demanding—and yet he could be such a little boy, cute and endearing. She began to feel as if she shouldn't have pushed him away so harshly and, in a moment of weakness, she leaned in and took his hand. What happened next, whether against the rules of Transition or not, was predictable if anyone knew Joe, because the next moment he was kissing her—up there in the choir balcony—and she didn't resist at all. But, as had happened before, some force that neither of them could predict broke the spell between them and they melted away, the kiss forever suspended into a space Joe and Alanna could not, did not, occupy.

FIVE

Emma awoke in the early morning to the chiming of church bells. She was stretched out under a puff of feather quilts in the bed of Colin MacGregor.

Or ... at least the bed Colin was staying in while he lived at his aunt's house awaiting his divorce. Emma rolled over in the snug nest and listened for sounds of movement and activity below her. It was bad enough she'd crashed in on Aileen and Brodie unexpectedly on Christmas Eve, but at least she could let them have their holiday breakfast together without her presence making things awkward.

Besides, it was nice to just lie here in Colin's bed, to imagine she could sense his presence, to observe his room at her leisure.

He obviously had only planned to be here on a temporary basis, for there were very few clues spread about the room. A rough woolen coat thrown over the back of a rocker. A copy of a recent political thriller on the bedside stand. Postcards pinned to the wall, most probably souvenirs from the places Colin had traveled throughout the years: a collection of pyramids, castles, and pagodas. A photograph of a little girl who seemed to be about a year old. Obviously his daughter, although she looked nothing like Colin or the rest of the MacGregor clan. Colin had jet black hair; she remembered that clearly enough. Curly and always a bit unruly looking. Eyes as blue as a jay's feather, a wry smile that Emma remembered always made her feel like he was teasing her. He was quick to step when he walked while his frame seemed too slender for a boy who'd grown up doing farm work. Emma could only conclude that the child in the picture frame resembled her mother. The mysterious almost-ex-wife who thought she could handle the simple country life of Alloway and then found it didn't suit her at all. Emma tried to picture such a woman. Was she some sort of sophisticate who thought she could draw Colin away from his roots? What had gone wrong in their marriage? And why had they married in the first place? Again Emma studied the photo of the little girl. Maybe the child had been the reason they'd married.

Emma pushed herself from the bed and wandered to the closet. The clothes inside, neatly lined on hangers, showed that Colin was still slim, still had a penchant for dark American jeans and white cotton T-shirts. Still trying to be James Dean or maybe Bruce Springsteen, Emma thought. Still trying to be a little tough and a little cool.

Beyond that, not much. Just the room of a man who was just passing through, who didn't plan to stay long. Emma wondered why he was rooming with his aunt and cousin at all. But then again, Alloway didn't seem to have any apartment complexes or condos. From what she'd seen driving in, a few rows of well-tended cottages was pretty much it. Of course, she hadn't seen everything and it had been dark.

From below her, she could hear the sound of clanging dishes and Aileen's sweet high voice, singing a carol. They had probably finished their family breakfast, so she decided to go down and fix herself a piece of toast. At least she had a bathrobe in her suitcase, something she'd felt she'd need during the school tour, when she'd sometimes roomed with students. At home, Emma usually slept in cotton pajamas.

When she entered the kitchen a few minutes later, the robe firmly tied around her waist, she found Aileen still at the sink. And despite her insistence that a mere piece of toast would be plenty, Aileen would have none of it. Within minutes she'd whipped up a fluffy omelet with cheese and ham. As Emma dug in, she realized that she was starving. When was the last time she'd eaten? Lunch yesterday in Gatwick Airport?

"You didn't have to hold breakfast for me," she said, gulping down her apple juice. "You must have thought I was going to sleep forever."

"Yes, indeed, I was almost ready to send Brodie 'round to knock you up," Aileen said airily, pouring herself a mug of tea.

"Knock me up?"

"Knock on the door and wake you," Aileen said, "But he convinced me to let you have your sleep."

"Oh. Oh, of course. 'Knocking people up' means something different in the States." Emma frowned down at her plate. Brodie must not have been terribly eager for her company at the breakfast table if he had urged his mother to let Emma sleep in. "I feel like I'm causing you all kinds of trouble," she added guiltily between bites. "Last night they said that people in the town rented out rooms for New Year's. Have I taken a bed you've promised to someone else?"

"Oh no, my dear, I wasn't planning for boarders. Colin moved into the guest room a few months back, as you've undoubtedly noticed. And when he returns from London, he can share quarters with Brodie. 'Tis truly no trouble."

"I guess that's his little girl in the picture. She's darling."

48

"An angel," Aileen promptly confirmed. "Perhaps I'm talking out of turn, but it's Colin's aim to ultimately gain child arrangement orders over the child. You know, dear, I believe you Americans call it 'custody'? Her mother insisted on dragging the child to London, which anyone knows isn't a fit place to bring up a baby, especially if a certain someone believes that she must immediately return to her law practice and put the poor little lamb in a childmind center. What do you call that?"

"Day care?"

"Yes, put the little darling into day care so that a certain someone can have her big important career. Not that I'm talking out of turn, mind you."

Emma grinned. Aileen would clearly be her best source on what was really up with Colin. "Alloway seems an ideal place to raise a child," she ventured, a sentence that made Aileen literally clap her hands with enthusiasm.

"Isn't it, though? Clean, safe streets, neighbors who are friends, family all about to keep a watchful eye on a tot. If she were here, you can bet I'd be a proper great-auntie."

"I have no doubt," said Emma. "But maybe someday you'll be a proper granny. What about Brodie? Any chance he'll be providing you with a daughter-in-law and grandchild anytime soon?"

"Ah, Brodie," Aileen said, sinking to the chair opposite Emma's. "The most loyal and devoted son a mother could wish for—maybe too much so. He loves the land, you see, my dear, and farming is a very demanding mistress. There's never been much time for girls and parties and such and, besides, Brodie's not a world traveler like our Colin. Should he decide he's ready for a wife and all that comes with it, where is he to find the lass? The selection in Alloway is rather limited."

"The girl I met last night was certainly pretty," Emma said. "What was her name? Skye?"

"Ah, Skye, as lovely as they come and twice as sweet as most." Aileen raised her chin and her eyes locked on Emma's, reminding her suddenly of the intense stare her Brodie had leveled at her last night over the chalice. Like mother, like son, Emma supposed. Both of them with the same soul-staring gaze.

"But that glance," Aileen continued softly, "has fallen on another."

Emma had wanted the full story, but now that she had it, she felt as if she'd been slapped. It was all clear enough without Aileen having to say any more. The girl who had played Fiona year after year had fallen in love with the boy who played Tommy, and who could blame her? Emma herself had become swept up in the very same pretend romance. A backstage kiss had grown in her mind until it had taken on power, far too much power—had lifted Colin to such a high status that no man she'd met since had ever been able to compete. But evidently Colin himself was not under the spell of *Brigadoon*. He craved the wider world, a world that contained lady lawyers from London. Hard, brilliant, glittering women that left poor Skye a poor second.

And Emma the school teacher was not much of a match for some competitive legal type probably with plans to make partner.

Aileen was still staring across the table at her with an expression that was direct, but not unsympathetic.

"Well," Emma said with a shaky laugh. "In my literature classes, I always teach my girls that there are two ways for a story to begin. Either someone takes a trip or a stranger comes to town."

"And here we have both," said Aileen, chuckling as she leaned forward to wrap her hands around a mug of steaming tea. "Our Colin has gone on a trip to London and then we have Emma, a stranger come to Alloway."

"I suppose," said Emma, attempting to sound careless and unconcerned as she scooped in the last bite of omelet. "Where is Brodie, anyway?"

"Out and about, if you can believe it so early on a Christmas morning. Now promise you won't be scandalized, but in Alloway we celebrate the holiday on the Eve, just as you saw last night. And on Christmas Day we begin to build the set for *Brigadoon*. Don't judge us too harshly, my dear," she went on, although Emma hadn't uttered a word. "We only have a week to get it all ready, and building the set is a tradition in its own right. The whole town comes together and we all bring covered dishes for a catch-all sort of dinner and it's really quite fun. They do the frame first, which is why Brodie is already at the schoolhouse, along with any other able-bodied man in the village. We ladies come together later for the painting and the set dressing, that sort of thing. You'll join us, will you not?"

"Oh, I'd love to," Emma said, with genuine enthusiasm. "Building and striking the set were my favorite parts of drama class, although I'm sure that makes me sound like a dreadful nerd. But you're right, it's so much fun when everyone works together, the whole cast and crew. And can I help you with the covered dish? I make an excellent chili."

"Chili?"

"Sort of an American stew," Emma said, making a mental note to leave out the spicier ingredients. Which shouldn't be a problem. There probably wasn't a jalapeno or poblano pepper within a hundred miles of Alloway.

"It's time for us to tell her," Joe said.

"Why? She doesn't seem to need our help. In fact, she seems to have landed herself in paradise."

"Paradise?" Joe said with a snort. The two had used the manifest again and were now somewhere among the cottage rafters, gazing down at Aunt Aileen and Emma, sipping tea and talking in the kitchen like old gal pals. This Wish Granters stuff was a funny business. Sometimes they moved among humans as equals, fully visible and participating in the Earthly existence. At other times they were almost spirits, floating unseen above their clients, observing but not participating. But they were not spirits. Not yet, at least. Joe, for one, didn't believe in such nonsense. Then again, there they were, unseen at times, visible at others, a contradiction no matter which way he viewed the situation.

"It seems we've landed her in a dead zone. As far as the mythical Colin is concerned. He sounds like a real "love 'em and leave 'em" kind of guy," Joe continued. "It's a mystery to me how women can get so fixated on one guy they kissed one time when they were barely out of grade school. What does this Colin have going for him anyway?"

"You just don't understand how women think," Alanna told him as she watched the two below. "A young girl can feel her first kiss is so special that she'll keep it locked away like a mother does with her baby's first curl. It's like someone whispers the first words of love and you've never heard them before. It means you're growing up, that you're special. Oh, how can I explain it to you?"

"You can't. I just don't get it."

"Well, I've heard guys talk about their 'first time' and they seem to get off on that pretty much the same way."

"That's different," Joe grinned. "That's something that actually happened."

"It is no different. That's where you're wrong. Except that, for a guy, it means conquest. And, for a girl, a kiss means she's really cared for. That a boy cares about her."

"No matter what *she* thinks, *I* think it's time to tell her what we're doing here and how she got to this little nowhere town. She ought to know that granting her wish to see Mr. Magical Kiss Colin again might come at a price."

"Could you possibly be any more gloomy?" Alanna sighed. "It's Christmas, for heaven's sake. Let's give her one more day of innocence. Let her make her chili and take it to the theater. What could be the harm in that?"

But Joe was right. This wish granting business wouldn't come without consequences or complications. One wish granted would not solve an entire puzzle.

The Alloway Players presented their annual performance of *Brigadoon* in the school's auditorium, which was located just behind the village church. Since the town did the same play year after year, they had the set building pretty much down to a science and, by the time

Aunt Aileen and Emma arrived, just after noon, the primary structure was already in place. Even without the walls and set decoration, Emma recognized at once the locales each part of the stage was meant to represent. The village green, the Campbell cottage, the heathery heath where Fiona and Tommy danced and sang and fell in love.

She walked to the makeshift table—a series of planks stretched across two sawhorses—and eased her bowl of highly-modified chili among the other dishes. Quite a spread had already been assembled, and she realized that the set building was really just an excuse for the whole town to spend Christmas afternoon together. Someone was seated at the piano and Christmas carols rang out through the air, occasionally accompanied by snatches of other songs. Emma looked up at the scaffolding. Brodie was perched near the top, nailing up the façade of the church steeple.

"What did you do for the bagpipes?"

"Hmm?" she said, turning to see Skye beside her.

"In the wedding scene in the play,' Skye said. "Did you have enough bagpipers in the States to lead the wedding couple in with a proper march?"

"Oh," Emma said, with a laugh. "I'm afraid we had to use a recording."

"Sacrilege," Skye said with a delicate shudder and for a moment Emma wondered if she was serious. She started to explain that this had been a small high school in Pennsylvania, an area not exactly known for skill with bagpipes, but then the girl's face split into a grin and she realized she was teasing.

"Yes, it was sacrilege," Emma said with a laugh. "And I'm sure it all seemed like a hopelessly amateur production to Colin who grew up seeing it done exactly right. What year did he start playing the lead?"

"He was seventeen and I was sixteen the first year we were Fiona and Tommy," Skye said and smiled a crooked little smile before turning to help a woman who'd just arrived with squirming twin toddlers. Emma added up the years. So Colin had assumed the lead role in the village play the year after he'd returned to town from his year of school in America. The first time he'd played Tommy had been with her. What did it mean, she wondered. Or maybe it meant nothing. She was dreamily replaying the events of so long ago when the Reverend Dunn approached, a full array of costumes draped from his arms.

"Delighted to see you, dear lass," he said. "I trust you spent a pleasant night with Aileen."

"She filled me to bursting with breakfast," Emma said with a laugh. "Do you need help with the costumes?"

"We wash them of course after each performance," said Dunn. "But I'm afraid they get a bit wrinkled and dusty during a year in storage. Will you help me beat them out a bit? Aye, it's a job each year to put on a full performance. I suppose real theater people have it easier with the same performance every night. We seem to be inventing the show almost anew each time, and I can say each year some unexpected thing occurs that sends us all round the bend."

"Let me help with this at least," Emma said, taking the first dress from the top of the pile. It was the character Fiona's dress. Bright red to stand out in the crowd scenes, embellished with a plaid sash from shoulder to waist. Someone had taken a great deal of care with its construction, and the cloth was soft to the touch. Emma couldn't resist holding it up to herself like an understudy imagining opening night. She caught Reverend Dunn watching her with a bemused look. His ruddy cheeks and eyes crinkled at the corners told her he understood how she felt. She wondered what the older man thought of her, really. Coming here, asking for Colin, holding this dress so longingly.

She carried it out to the school steps, where she used one of the sticks Dunn had given her to gently beat the velvet cloth. A bit of dust flew but, as she continued to pound, the wrinkles began to fall out, almost as well as if she'd been home with her steamer. The activity warmed her in the cold, crisp air.

While concentrating on the dress, she didn't notice Brodie come through the school door. It wasn't until he leaned against the stone wall in front of the school, took out his pipe, lit it, and sucked to get the tobacco lit that Emma realized she was no longer alone. She glanced over at him and smiled, a little tentative smile, because so far he had said not two words to her. So he smoked, did he? She didn't even know any American man who still smoked. Still, she supposed, when in Alloway ...

"She loves him, you know."

It was an abrupt statement that startled her for its suddenness as well as its content. Emma knew who he meant. In fact, both of them. She waited before answering. There was a challenge in the way he said it, almost as if he wanted her to tell him to go bite himself. But that wasn't Emma's style, although the thought whizzed through her mind at an astounding pace. Instead, she stopped beating the dress and turned to him full-on. Now was the moment she had dreaded. The moment when someone would ask what she was really doing there.

Why she had come all this way. Why she had asked for Colin last night and why, after so many years, she would venture out in the dead of winter on such an excursion. So far no one had asked her any of these questions. Maybe she would have been happy to answer them, or at least not surprised that they would want to know. But now this. It was not a question about her. He seemed to have no interest in her motives.

"I see," she said, which was really not saying much at all. "And you're telling me this because ..."

Brodie shrugged, inhaled deeply from his pipe so the bowl glowed with a red-hot center that Emma could see from across the steps. She shivered. Now that she had quit beating the dress, she felt the chill air.

She took a further step and asked, "Is that your way of saying I shouldn't have come here?"

Brodie continued puffing absently on his pipe. Now Emma began to feel a bit annoyed. What business was it of his why she had come or who she was or how she felt? So she tried a bolder tack.

"Besides," she went on, since Brodie didn't answer. And she thought: Damn, he's got a nerve. This relieved her of any last reserve and she spoke again, "If they were in love, why did he marry some lawyer from London?"

"Never said they were in love, did I?" He said it rather too harshly. "'They' is a very specific word, meaning more than one person. No, Skye was in love and Colin was restless. So when he brought Destiny from London to Alloway, we all thought ..."

"His wife's name is Destiny? That sounds more like a hooker than a lawyer," Emma snapped. She was surprised by the spite in her own voice. Brodie was looking at her so impassively that it was almost as if he hadn't understood what she was saying, and perhaps he hadn't. "A 'hooker' is the American term for a ..."

"I know what a hooker is," Brodie said calmly, a puff of smoke escaping the pipe, surrounding them with a rich scent of cherry and peat.

He was infuriating. Smug and arrogant, she thought. Like some old uncle warning her about the bad boy in town. But he had knocked the air out of her and now she felt like a collapsed balloon with all the hope for this escapade fading away. "I guess you're saying that Colin has already broken Skye's heart once and no one in Alloway wants to see it happen again."

"Maybe so," he said with a shrug. "But what should she have expected? The ladies all love Colin, do they not? And what do they get in return for all that? Better to steer clear of the whole business." He tamped his pipe against the wall and looked up at the sky. "Be dark soon enough. Chores won't do themselves, will they now?"

A shudder ran through Emma that had nothing to do with the December cold. This farmer with his pipe and knitted cap telling her she was one of many girls Colin had courted through the years. Not the prettiest or the smartest or the most memorable. Not even the most recent. And who had asked for his commentary anyway?

"Perhaps Skye should have taken the hint and begun to look elsewhere," she said. "Or is she waiting around for Colin's divorce to be final, for him to win custody of his little girl and come to his senses? To see that the love of his life was standing right before him all along?" As she said the words, it occurred to Emma that this was precisely Skye's hope. That a wandering Colin would realize there was nothing better out there than what he had all along right here in Alloway. It occurred to Emma that's precisely what would happen. Skye was beautiful and sweet. Why shouldn't Colin return to her?

The wind was rising. Emma felt its bite. The dress was back to its performance-ready state. There was nothing to hold her on the steps here now.

"No," Brodie said calmly. "No matter what she might hope, Skye knows Colin's heart. He's never been the sort to marry the girl next door. He's always thought of himself doing grand things with grand people. We're part of the Earth here. That's not for Colin."

"Excuse me," Emma said. She pulled the door open. As she walked back toward the auditorium, she struggled to control her shaking hands and not let the tears that now pricked at the corners of her eyes fall down her cheeks. If Brodie had wanted to destroy her confidence, he couldn't have done a more thorough job. She thought back to sixteen-year-old Colin, a boy so determined to see the world that he'd flown halfway around the globe to an unknown town in rural Pennsylvania. Colin, the man who had traveled to Italy, Egypt, and Japan, who had brought home a wife from London. Colin—who had undoubtedly known and loved many women—had enjoyed she could not know how many love affairs since their backstage kiss.

But perhaps Brodie was only speaking out of spite. Especially if his own life had been constricted by the family farm and a mother who depended on him. Then of course he would envy his more glamorous cousin. And what about that comment about all the ladies loving Colin? This must be a source of resentment between the two of them.

Resolutely, Emma made her way back to the auditorium. Coming to Alloway wasn't working out exactly as she'd planned, but she was here now, wasn't she? Only days away from seeing Colin again and, whatever happened, she wasn't going to let his pipe-smoking, sheep-herding cousin run her off before she got her chance. She walked down the auditorium aisle and onto the stage, then hung Fiona's dress on a rack before turning to the next costume from the box. It was the bridal gown the character Jean would wear in the wedding scene.

"Come, lass," Dunn was saying to Skye. "It's your job to hang the bell and then we'll all have our dinner."

A boy brushed by with a ladder and set it up in front of the painted church. Someone else had gotten out a real silver church bell—a large and very accurate-looking prop. Evidently part of the Alloway Players production of Brigadoon was a real, ringing church bell to announce the wedding scene; and, just as evidently, it was tradition for the girl who played Fiona to hang that bell. Emma and the whole group watched as the young boy held the ladder while Skye climbed.

"Here's to another successful performance," Dunn called out grandly. It dawned on Emma that he was also the director of the play, the one who kept the whole production running smoothly. "Another bountiful year with enough funds to expand the school library."

"Hear, hear," someone else echoed. The town matrons—who had already lined up behind the food table in anticipation of the rush to follow—clapped with enthusiasm.

Skye reached down to take the bell from the boy and turned to hang it. Emma sighed. Perhaps Brodie was right. Why had she come? Why had she forced her way into this perfect little scene, into this world that was so whole and intact without her? They certainly didn't need her here.

60

The matching veil for the bridal dress she was to refresh next was stuck in the box, wedged beneath the costume below it. Emma tugged at it slightly.

On the ladder, Skye carefully stretched up toward the bell tower.

Damn. That veil was really jammed in there. Emma pulled a little harder.

The door in the back of the auditorium opened. Brodie walked in, stuffing his pipe into his jacket pocket.

The people on stage waited and watched in silence as Skye reached up to hang the bell.

Emma jerked at the wedding dress. Everyone clapped as the bell transferred from Fiona's hands to its proper position. And then, just in that moment, the veil came loose from the clothes below it, causing Emma's arm to fly out with a jerk. She stumbled. Almost caught herself. From the corner of her eye she could see Brodie, starting toward her, his face set in a frown.

She was righted. No, not quite, still off balance, she reached her hand out, grabbed the first thing she could find, which was the ladder.

Emma stumbled into the ladder, the wedding dress falling on top of her. Skye swayed and clutched the top of the ladder, letting out a little scream. The young boy tried to steady it. The ladies gasped from behind their tables. Brodie ran the rest of the aisle and leaped to the stage, his arms outstretched.

But it was too late. The ladder pitched from the stage and crashed into the floor, taking the fair Skye McFae along with it.

SIX

"I know you work in mysterious ways and all that," Joe said, "but this seems a bit much. Knocking some poor girl off a ladder and breaking her leg just so Emma can play the part of Fiona."

Joe and Alanna had manifested again, and this time Morgan had appeared where they were seated in the back of the auditorium, still invisible to the citizens of Alloway, who were dashing back and forth up the aisle in a panic. They had called for an ambulance, which would be coming from the nearby village of Ayr, but considering the fact it was a snowy Christmas afternoon, apparently no one was holding out hope that it would arrive anytime soon. The focus of the crowd was keeping Skye as comfortable as possible—a solution that seemed to involve pillows, prayers, and a bottle of brandy.

Morgan shook his head. "Not my doing, I assure you. That was simply a random accident, as far as I know at this time. Of course, as events unfold, that opinion is open to reconsideration."

Morgan could be so vague at times that Joe would get agitated and want to cross-examine him.

"What do you base that assessment on?" he asked, but Alanna broke in before Morgan could answer.

"What makes you so sure Emma will play the part of Fiona?" Alanna asked. "She's feeling so guilty that she may just depart Alloway before nightfall."

"Honestly," Joe said, shaking his head. "It's like you've never seen a chick flick. Boom goes the ladder and

Skye's on the floor with her leg doubled back like a sacked NFL quarterback." He shook a finger at Morgan. "And I'm still not convinced you didn't have something to do with all this. Think about it: A strange American wanders into town and the next thing you know the darling of whole village goes flying. No wonder everyone in Europe hates us."

"It wasn't Emma's fault," Alanna said stonily. "You're acting as if she planned for Skye to fall."

"Maybe not, but let's face facts," Joe said. "It's a matter of days until the play is scheduled, and Emma knows the part. Who else will they turn to? And that means she'll be sitting there waiting for Colin when he comes back from London, already wearing her red costume with the plaid sash."

"I thought you didn't like chick flicks. So how do you know so much about them?" Alanna asked, for his read of the situation was undoubtedly accurate.

"I'm not sure," Joe said slowly. "I must have had a girlfriend once and she must have dragged me to them." His voice was wistful and a little sad. Alanna glanced at him, but he was still staring straight ahead at the stage, where the town was gathered around Skye as Emma sobbed in the wings.

"All I know," Joe went on, sounding more like himself, "is that it seems like this case should be a slam dunk. You know, it's such a simple little wish: find a guy and kiss him. Should be a quick in and out and then we're on to the next assignment. But ever since we've arrived here at MacHootersville, it's been one complication after another, and I really don't have time for this girl-falls-off-a-ladder, start-of-a-Lifetime movie kind of crap. Next thing you know there's going to be a reunion between twins separated at birth or some guy's going to get paralyzed in a boating accident and his loving girlfriend will sacrifice all to tend him until the end of time."

Of the two stories going on simultaneously in this building, Alanna wasn't sure which one to follow. She and Joe would sometimes get glimpses of memory from their own lives. Always in odd ways and unpredictable times. Joe seemed to be having one now. During their previous case, Joe had concluded that he'd been a lawyer, that he had worked with a partner, and that something horrible must have happened to that partner. Something Joe was unable to prevent. Beyond that was only the dark night of forgetfulness, but Alanna supposed that even these small shards of memory were pulling him back. Because, with each day that passed, Joe seemed more determined to earn his way home to Earth, even if he didn't totally understand how to do it or even what would be waiting for him there if he managed to return. Now he'd had a new flicker of recollection: being dragged into chick flicks with a girlfriend. But it was impossible to say whether or not this was a woman he'd loved at the time of his accident or someone from his distant past. Joe became more of an enigma to Alanna as time passed. He must have had someone in his life. A guy like Joe wouldn't remain single. Or maybe he was one of those men who could never commit to just one woman. A pollen gatherer and seed spreader. Well, what did it matter now? They were here and their lives on Earth were done.

Her own story wasn't much clearer. There had definitely been a fiancé for, at various times during their first case, she'd remembered an engagement ring. There was also a distinct memory of luxury surrounding her. The

64

thought of having been some rich bitch made her feel distraught, and she dismissed the notion whenever it surfaced, figuring she couldn't be feeling the way she did now if she'd been some self-involved little princess back then.

Still, there were the vague impressions of a life of luxury. Flying first class, champagne, the feel of silk against her skin, and one sense that she couldn't quite picture clearly of a place where she was supposed to be. A place with crystal champagne flutes and lots of flowers. But the real mystery was: If her life had been so great, why wasn't she eager to return to it? Because every time Joe talked about going back, Alanna had felt a tightness in her chest. She didn't want to reclaim her life, but she wasn't precisely sure why.

Not all of her recaptured memories had been so pleasant. She'd also had flashes of blood and pain, of lying in a hospital bed alone. And there was the continual sense that the life she'd left on Earth had been all laid out for her, leaving her no room to breathe. She wanted to remember it all. But, in another way, she didn't.

So here they were. A lawyer who had lost his partner through violence, who was determined to return and rectify the situation. A girl who'd known love and money but to whom something bad had evidently happened. Bad enough that she only wanted to go forward, to earn her way through Transition and to whatever lay beyond. Those were the stories of Joe and Alanna. Complicated and disturbing. Unresolved and in limbo. And there was Morgan, reminding them to stay on course where they were now. Alanna thought, at some point, that Morgan knew much more than they did, so putting her trust in him was the only viable option. Stay focused on their task.

Help the person they'd been sent to help. Trust Morgan to do right by everyone. Anyway, they didn't seem to have much choice.

The story of Emma was the one that really mattered, at least for now. And Emma was sitting down on the steps leading from the stage with her face buried in her hands.

"What happens if she does leave?" Joe asked Morgan. "If she goes back to London without ever having seen Colin? Do we still get credit for this case?"

Morgan gave his customary little chuckle, the one that he always used to show Joe and Alanna that they were being especially dense. "Why do you insist on believing it's a matter of earning your way to one place or another?" he asked. "You're not a Boy Scout collecting badges, or a schoolteacher saving for retirement."

"When we first met you up in Transition, you explained that these cases are how we get back to Earth," Joe said sharply. "God, man, you've told us so little that it seems like you could at least be consistent with what you do say."

"The cases are what determine when you leave Transition, but it's not as numerical as you think," said Morgan. "It's not a matter of twenty wishes granted and then you move on. Some Wish Granters only handle a case or two ... others stay with us much longer. You'll know when it's time, when you've learned what you're meant to learn."

Joe sputtered in indignation. He liked things clean and laid out. Tell him he has to grant a million wishes. He'd be fine with that. At least he'd know he had nine hundred ninety-nine thousand nine hundred ninety-seven more miserable women left to help. But tell him that there was no definite point in the future when he'd be allowed back—that he himself would know when the time was right—was the equivalent of telling Joe he was in Hell. If there was any shred of negotiation strategy he could employ, Joe would always go for it.

"So it's all the same to us, if she goes or if she stays?" Joe finally said. "We're in exactly the same situation whether Emma falls into Colin's arms or if she flies on home to Providence?"

Morgan, watching the scene below, slowly turned to Joe and asked, "Are you?"

"No," Alanna said resolutely. "We've come to help this girl find her first love and we're going to complete the task, no matter where it takes us. So far we haven't done anything but watch her stumble her way into a crisis. It's time we tell her who we are and why we're here."

"What are we going to do, jump out and say, 'Boo'?" Joe pointed out. "She can't see us." The most frustrating thing about this Wish Granter business—besides that there was no telling how long it would take to work their way through it—was that sometimes their manifesting left them in human form and sometimes it didn't. Joe felt sure there had to be some way to control when they were visible and when they were not, but so far he hadn't found the right button.

"Alanna's right," Morgan said. "Our little friend Emma is feeling very guilty right now, and nothing can blind a human to his or her true potential quite like guilt. So it's time for us to give the situation a little nudge." Joe felt a brief shimmering sensation pass through his body and then Morgan stood and walked down the aisle.

"Did someone call a cab?" he asked pleasantly.

"Praise the Lord," said Aunt Aileen. "We rang for an ambulance but the roads are impassable. However did you get through?"

"Well, I'm not an ambulance, but I can certainly take this young lady to Ayr," Morgan said, not bothering to answer an unanswerable question. And that was enough to spring the men clustered around Skye into action, as they stretched her out on a quilt as a makeshift gurney. She cried out in pain when they tried to lift her. But when Morgan stooped to grab the edges of the quilt, Skye sank back, and they lifted her gently as if she was a broken bird. She managed a shaky smile as the group carried her down the aisle and out of the front of the auditorium to Morgan's waiting cab.

Only Emma was left on the stage. Teary-eyed and, once again, alone.

SEVEN

*P*oor Emma, Alanna thought as she walked toward her. *But this isn't the end, Emma, girl, now that we've gotten the go-ahead to help you.*

Emma looked up, almost by some animal instinct—the way a trapped raccoon that realizes there's no way out calms down and accepts its fate. Still, for an instant, confusion flittered across her tear-stained face, and it must have seemed wholly implausible at this particular time for someone she'd only briefly met and spoken with at an airport—a place known for its fleeting and usually meaningless encounters—to be here, in this church at this moment.

"What are you doing here?" For a span of time just brief enough for paranoia to creep in, Emma speculated that maybe she was being followed. But for what reason, she couldn't guess. "I thought you were spending Christmas in Edinburgh."

Alanna reached out a hand to help Emma stand. "Well, there's rather a long story about that. Where's your coat and hat? This is my friend Joe, and we'd like you to take a walk with us."

"I'm not sure I want to go walking right now. Did you happen to see what happened? It was all my fault. These people; I mean, when they get back, they'll probably want to string me up. And they've been so nice to me. Welcomed me like a family member. Oh God, I've never felt more humiliated."

"We saw the whole thing," Joe said. He could be soft spoken and comforting. It was another quality that Alanna found perplexing about Joe. And appealing.

"How?" Emma looked up at him and then at Alanna. "Where were you? I never saw you in here."

"That's part of what we want to talk about. Come on," Joe added. "It'll do you good to get out of here. They won't be back for some time, and you need some air to clean out the cobwebs. None of this was your fault. You'll see. Everything will be fine."

Emma was still confused, but Joe's argument—and that's what it was—made sense. Two Americans here? At Christmas? It was too much to think about, and she tried to reason that the fall was just an accident that could have happened to anyone. A walk in the fresh air would do her good. And, as soon as that strange cabbie guy got back from taking Skye to the hospital, she'd talk him into driving her back to the airport. That would be the best thing all around. She'd be on a plane in a day or two at the most and back home where things made sense. And no more thinking about Colin and what might have been.

With a nod toward Joe, she gathered her coat, hat, scarf, and gloves and the three of them picked their unsteady way down the school steps and into the icy street. It was just after four p.m. according to the clock on the church steeple, but the sun was already beginning to set, turning the open fields and yards into a blanket of wildly glittery crystals in shades of yellow and mauve. The streets were empty. Apparently, everyone in Alloway was involved in getting Skye transported to that hospital in Ayr.

"It's beautiful, isn't it?" Alanna ventured softly.

Emma nodded and wiped her eyes. "When I first got here, I thought it looked like one of those pictures on a jigsaw puzzle box."

"Last night?"

"Was it," Emma said shakily. "Was it really just last night?"

"Have you seen the bridge yet?" Joe asked. "It's what the town is famous for, right? The bridge over the river Doon?"

"No, I haven't," said Emma. "I arrived in darkness and today I've been rather, well, occupied."

Joe stepped between the two women and grandly offered an arm to each. "Then that's our destination. Ladies ..." and they locked arms.

"I don't understand," Emma said, although the three began their slippery journey down the street. "Are you two here to see the play? I know Aileen said people come into town for the performance, but that's almost a week away. And now, thanks to me, I don't know if there will even be a ..."

"What I'm about to tell you is going to sound fantastical," Alanna said. "But try to see it as a good thing, a chance to make all this turn out right."

Emma looked at her skeptically, her blue eyes barely visible over the top of her soft pink scarf.

"Do you remember back in the airport in London when you told me that the thing you wanted most in life was to find Colin? That was a wish, and a wish is a very powerful thing. It has the power to change your present reality."

"That's right," Joe continued. "Alanna and I are part of a group called The Wish Granters. We're assigned certain cases, such as yourself, women who want

71

something passionately. It's our job to help them make that wish a reality."

Emma stopped short in the street. "You think I asked for this? That I wanted Skye to get hurt?" She sounded angry and then, when what Joe had said slowly began to register, she looked from him to Alanna as if they had suddenly begun speaking in tongues.

"No, not at all," Alanna assured her. "But as we learned with our first case, the wish sets all kinds of forces into motion, most of them unforeseen. We can't control any of that; we just have to follow wherever the wish leads us and have ... faith, I suppose."

"I don't understand," Emma began. "Your first case? What are you talking about? Are you making fun of me? Because if you are ... if you followed me all the way up here from the London airport, well that's just really sick and weird."

"Emma," Alanna drew in a deep breath and exhaled a cloud of warm vapor. "We're here to help you make your wish a reality. Honestly. We didn't meet at the airport by chance. We were sent to help you. Please believe us. We are your Wish Granters."

"Who pays you?" Emma still looked skeptical. She stamped her feet in the snow to keep the circulation going.

"Nobody," Joe said shortly.

"Then why do you do it?"

"I've wondered that myself," Joe said.

"It's our mission," Alanna said, shooting him a warning glance. "We have no choice in the matter. You'll just have to accept it. You have no choice either. And we wouldn't be here if you didn't want your wish in a deep and important way."

72

Emma began walking again. She hadn't openly called them liars or fools but she was far from convinced. "So I'm supposed to see this as some sort of Christmas miracle."

"If it helps you to buy into it," said Joe. "Even though it looks like we're going to be working all year long. Look, we know all you want to do is see Colin. Maybe kiss him, maybe more. That was the wish and that's what we'll help you get. Skye getting hurt was just—well, I don't think it was entirely an accident; I think it's part of what had to happen for the wish to be granted. That's the thing. When our last client made her wish, it sounded simple and straightforward. Wishes always do, I guess. But in the process of living out the wish, things got very complicated ..."

"Wait a minute," Emma said sharply. "Alanna said 'first case' and you said, 'last client.'" Are you saying you've done this before? With two different people?"

Joe and Alanna glanced at each other.

"Correct," Joe finally said. "Okay, so we're not the most experienced Wish Granters. We've had just two wishes to grant before yours. But they worked out fine. You'll just have to trust us." Joe thought about adding Morgan to the explanation to show they weren't flying completely solo. But maybe that wasn't allowed. And anyway, Morgan never clarified much of anything, so Joe decided it was better to keep that part from Emma.

After a few minutes of silence, Emma said, "Great. I've got trainee Wish Granters on the case. No wonder Skye fell off the ladder." She frowned again, as another thought hit her.

"That weird cab driver," she said. "He works for you too, doesn't he?"

Joe peered at Emma in the fading light. Well, so she had guessed it anyway. Now it was out in the open, he felt a bit relieved—that the entire burden didn't rest on their shoulders alone.

"Actually, we work for him," Alanna said. "But yes, his name is Morgan. He's a very important part of this mission. And if it makes you feel better, he's far more experienced with this sort of thing than we are."

"I don't mean to be rude," Emma said. "But I can't really see what you guys have done so far other than follow me to Alloway. Morgan is a good, cheap, fast cab driver who always seems to be there when you need him and yeah, that's a miracle. But, otherwise, where's the magic?"

"Look," said Joe. "There's the bridge."

They had come to the end of Alloway's main street and stood gazing out over the little stone bridge that led out of town. The river beneath it was half-frozen and glowed pink and purple with the setting sun. The three made their way up the small rise and stood at the top of the bridge. In one direction lay the town, as still as the set of a play when all the actors have departed. In the other direction was the winding road which led to Ayr and further to Edinburgh, to the airport, and the world beyond.

"Did Colin often stand on this bridge, do you think?" Alanna asked quietly.

"I imagine," Emma said. Her mood had shifted, and her voice was also soft. "He always said he'd travel the world and, judging by the postcards on his wall, I'd say he did. Yet he always came back here."

"I wonder why," Joe said.

"Are you joking?" Alanna said. "This is the most beautiful little village I've ever seen, and the most

74

charming people. The mystery isn't why he came home; it's why he would ever leave in the first place."

Before either Joe or Emma could answer, all three of them became aware of a fourth presence, a figure walking from the town toward the bridge. Clearly a man, but bundled so tightly against the weather that it took them a minute to recognize him as Brodie. Where they had picked their way slowly down the street, he strode with confidence through the snow and stopped at the base of the bridge, where he looked up at Emma.

"Here you are," he said softly. "My mum was afraid you'd fled back to London."

"I should leave," Emma said. "I stumble into town unannounced in the middle of the night before Christmas and everyone takes me in, is so incredibly kind. Especially your mother. And I repay your kindness by ruining your play."

"The play isn't ruined. Hasn't even happened yet, has it? And how can something that hasn't yet happened be ruined?"

Good point, thought Joe.

Emma sniffled, "I broke your Fiona."

Brodie's eyes pointedly shifted to Joe and Alanna and Emma seemed to suddenly remember they were standing there. "Oh, sorry," she said. "This is Alanna and Joe. They're ... they're friends of mine from America and they came to see the play."

"Brodie, your town is charming," Alanna said. She recognized her mistake immediately. Emma had never finished her introduction, had never said Brodie's name. For a second she felt stricken as a fleeting thought that they might be discovered, questioned, with the whole assignment unraveling because of her careless comment, but he didn't appear to notice anything odd, only smiled with pride. Alanna quickly recovered and smiled back.

"See there," he said. "Our monument in honor of the poet Robert Burns. You've heard of him, haven't you, in America, yet?" He walked the few steps toward Alanna, took Alanna's arm and led her down the bridge and over to where they could look at the rather grand Grecian-style temple with nine pillars surrounded by snow-covered gardens that wound up the hill and surrounded it.

"It's certainly in contrast to his humble house in town," Alanna said.

"Aye, that 'tis." Brodie lit his pipe and the two of them walked further down the bridge to the river Doon below and fell into conversation about the poem called "Tam O'Shanter."

Brodie's soft voice, along with the rich, sweet scent of tobacco, drifted back up to Emma and Joe on the bridge.

When chapman billies leave the street,
And drouthy neebors neebors meet,
As market-days are wearing late,
And folk begin to tak the gate;
While we sit bousin, at the nappy,
And gettin fou and unco happy,
We think na on the lang Scots miles,
The mosses, waters, slaps, and stiles,
That lie between us and our hame,
Whare sits our sulky, sullen dame,
Gathering her brows like gathering storm,
Nursing her wrath to keep it warm.*

Joe leaned across the wall of the bridge and clasped his hands. The sun had fallen even further, the pink and gold of the water giving way to colors of gray and blue as shadows draped themselves around the shoulders of Alloway. He and Emma listened to Brodie recite the poem, like music in the evening air around them.

He heard Alanna ask Brodie, "What does the poem mean?"

Brodie puffed on his pipe as if searching for the answer. Then he took it from his mouth and stared at the river.

"Well, 'tis about a man named Tom—'Tam' in the Gaelic, you see—a cautionary tale about witches and warlocks and the devil. About what can happen to a man should he drink too much and go carousing. Also I suppose 'tis a kind of warning about the countryside hereabout. It tells tales of wild abandonment, about pleasures and temptations of a less-than-Earthly sort. It seems to me, Mr. Burns saw some frightening things in his drinking days as he wandered home across this very bridge. Aye, the Devil can take many a form."

"Thanks for calling us 'friends from America,'" Joe said to Emma. "Does that mean you plan to stay here and see this thing through?"

"I'm not sure," Emma said. They heard the tinkle of Alanna's laughter and the deeper sound of Brodie's chuckle.

"The Scottish lad with the pipe and the curly dark hair is obviously charming Alanna off her keister," Joe said. "Is he much like his cousin?"

"Brodie's a bit rougher than Colin," Emma said, her eyes fixed on the river. "More countrified. But yeah, there's something similar."

"Morgan can drive us back to Edinburgh tonight if you want to go," Joe said. He didn't know why he said it. If Emma never met Colin, then this whole case would be a bust. But he didn't want her to feel trapped, and he had the sense she was already beginning to regret her wish.

The two of them turned, looked down at Alanna and Brodie beneath them in the glade. Brodie had scooped up a handful of snow and packed it into the perfect snowball and had then placed it into the outstretched palm of Robert Burns, and Alanna was doubled over with laughter as if this were the wittiest thing she had ever seen in her life.

"Hell, she might stay even if you go," Joe said. "I've never seen anybody go so head over heels about a place." Alanna was a mystery to him. She was beautiful and, yeah, he was attracted, but the things they liked were so different, their reactions so divergent. For the dozenth time, he wondered why Morgan had ever paired them.

"I have another question," Emma said, shuddering slightly in a breeze that had kicked up out of nowhere. She turned away from the bridge. "I don't want to be rude, but ..."

"Ask me. Anything."

"Are you alive or ... dead?"

Joe chuckled and took her arm. They began inching their way off the bridge, back toward Alanna and Brodie. "Believe it or not," he said, "I don't know."

Anywhere else, at any other time, Emma would have run for her life after being introduced to Alanna and Joe and told about granting wishes and not knowing the difference between being alive or dead. If they were spirits, well, she supposed this was the right place for them to appear. And if they weren't ... it was the wish that she could see Colin again, that powerful wish that kept her from running away back to a sterile airport and what passed for reality. As she walked, with her arm in Joe's, she felt a sense of peace that had been missing from her life so far. Always she had felt there must be something more than what you could see with your eyes. Perhaps her attachment to Colin was just a part of that. A thirst for something deeper.

EIGHT

The Reverend Dunn was adamant. "But you have to stay, my dear. You know the part, after all."

"It's been ten years since I said those lines," Emma protested. "And when it comes to the singing and dancing ..."

"You can learn it all again. Far faster the second time, I'd predict. We'll help you." Dunn clearly was not prepared to take no for an answer. He had already pulled the red dress that Fiona would wear throughout the play from the rack and was holding it out to Emma. "The ballet is the only difficult sequence, so we'll begin there."

The ballet. Her favorite part of *Brigadoon*: the scene where Fiona and Tommy danced on the Scottish hillsides. Or, more accurately, in her high school production, in front of a painted backdrop of heather and heath. Emma glanced at the half-decorated stage. Here in the Alloway production, they used real heather. Of course, the blooms had been dried for the winter production and then a group of local women had tied them carefully onto the plants, which had been dug up and potted for the play. The effect was that of a blooming field of heather.

Real heather and the real Colin. And an almost irresistible chance to step back in time. To once again feel Colin's hands around her waist, that soft exhalation he made as he lifted her, the moment where she hung in mid-air, looking down into his flashing dark eyes. Her singing voice was fine; she knew this. Nothing extraordinary, but Fiona only had one solo, and it was early in the play. Her acting, likewise, adequate. What had won her the part of Fiona back in eleventh grade had been her dancing. That and her undeniable chemistry with her leading man.

"Colin isn't even here to rehearse with me ..."

"Brodie can work with you until Colin returns on Friday," Dunn said firmly, bundling the red dress into her arms. "He's the double and he knows the part just fine."

"Double?"

"I think in America you call it a 'stand-in,'" Aunt Aileen broke in. "You have to remember, Reverend, the girl doesn't speak precisely the same language we do. Either way, he's done it for years, too, hasn't he? Ever since Colin took the role?"

"Well, of course he has," Joe said quietly to Alanna. "Doesn't something about this seem strange to you? Brodie patiently holding down the fort at home while Colin zips around having adventures, Brodie as the stand-in, the shoulder for all of Colin's cast-off girlfriends to cry on? He'd have to resent the hell out of his cousin."

"Some people are more comfortable being in the background," Alanna said.

"And the friends from America," Dunn was saying. "Another act of providence, I'm sure. "You'll lend aid as well, will you not?"

Alanna jumped, startled at suddenly being the center of attention. For a moment she had forgotten they were visible. Everyone they'd met since manifesting had taken their sudden appearance as absolutely normal. What with so many arriving for the play every year, and the tourists who visited the village to pay tribute to their hometown poet, two more Americans didn't seem to faze anyone.

"Of course," she said, recovering smoothly. "Joe and I will do everything we can to help you make *Brigadoon* a success."

The next day started with Alanna in a strange mood. She wasn't sure exactly what was bothering her, so she took her time showering and dressing, to give herself the chance to sort through it all.

When Emma had introduced them as friends from America, Aileen had thrown her arms wide and insisted on taking them into her home too. Brodie had agreed to sleep on the couch and thus give up his room to Alanna and Joe, whom everyone in town assumed were married. So they had gone home with Aileen, eaten dinner, told everyone goodnight and Merry Christmas, climbed the stairs, entered the small room together, looked at the bed and then at each other.

And then Joe had reluctantly, but tactfully, dematerialized. It was one of the mysteries of manifesting. Sometimes they knew where they were going to land and, at others, they simply evaporated for a time—appearing somewhere else, surprised by their own arrival.

It was all just one more puzzle in a world of puzzlement. At times on Earth, they certainly had bodies, and those bodies seemed to do everything that normal bodies do: eat, sleep, breathe, cry, laugh. Enjoy the pleasure of a shower, of water splashing over your shoulders and running down your back. Last night, Alanna had even sneezed in the presence of the holly on Aileen's table, something she had viewed as a noteworthy event. She hadn't had any plant allergies in her old body, so why had she sneezed now? Was she in a different body that only resembled the original? And if this were some sort of loaner body, only hers while she was on Wish Granter missions, wouldn't it be a perfect heavenly body, and thus not allergic to holly?

But, of course, a sprig of holly wasn't the real issue.

The real issue was sex. At least Joe had always claimed that was the big issue for him. Would he ever make love to a woman again? There were certain things about an Earthly existence—such as taxes, physical pain, and commutes from the suburbs of Boston—which Joe declared he was more than happy to say goodbye to. But there were other Earthly experiences—namely sex, sex, and sex—that he knew he would miss. Whenever Alanna and Joe had speculated on exactly where they were or what their time in Transition meant in terms of their humanity, Joe had always managed to steer the conversation back to a single thread: whether or not they were still capable of sex.

In some ways he was the most fascinating man she'd ever met—brave, smart, audacious, and loyal. But in other ways, he was a typical man. All roads led to sex and, more specifically, the possibilities of sex with Alanna. There had been so many times she had caught him staring at her with an expression that was easy to read. Could a few words of warning from Morgan really have changed him so completely?

For Alanna it was a little different. When Emma had told her about that kiss with Colin so many years ago, Emma's face had lit up, transported by the memory—and, it had occurred to Alanna, that memory was the way mortal beings were capable of their own sort of magical manifestation. For Emma had clearly been (even if just for a split second) back on that high school stage being kissed by the first boy who had ever moved her.

And in that moment, Alanna had a very precise thought: "Will I ever be kissed again? And will I ever know real romantic love?"

The difference between the two questions had pulled her up short, and as she rubbed herself dry with the towel and pulled on her jeans, Alanna ran the words back over in her mind. She wondered if she would ever be kissed again. A clear enough question. Then she wondered if she would ever know romantic love. There was no "again" at the end of that question. So Alanna was left with the vague sense that she had never really loved anyone. Or maybe that no one had loved her. Perhaps both. And a lawyer like Joe would have pounced on this inconsistency. If, during her twenty-eight years on Earth, Alanna had been kissed and had enjoyed it—but had never truly been in love—perhaps it was up to Joe to take the lead in that department. Joe, who had his own misgivings about his past on Earth, was an unlikely suitor for anything more than a brief, albeit pleasurable, encounter.

Here, alone in Brodie's room on the day after Christmas, Alanna wished she had another woman to discuss all this with. Being a Wish Granter could be a bit lonely at times, with only Joe and Morgan to talk to. She wouldn't begin to know how to raise this issue with them. She knew she'd been engaged on Earth, but had she not been in love with her fiancé? If she hadn't been in love with him, why had she agreed to marry him? Would she ever figure any of this out?

Maybe that's why I understand Brodie so well, Alanna thought, looking around the simple room. I was a stand-in my whole life, just like him, only I was a stand-in for myself. She was beginning to suspect that she had never really lived while she was alive, and this knowledge raised a lump in her throat. As emotionally precarious as Emma's situation was, at times Alanna recognized a feeling of envy. At least Emma knew what she wanted, even if it was something as simple as one more kiss. Still, her life held so many possibilities. She was entirely alive after all.

When Alanna finally dressed and went down the stairs, Joe was already seated at the table, wolfing down a breakfast better suited for a man about to go plow the fields than a tourist ready to explore a village that had only one street.

"Aileen was just telling me that Emma's agreed to play Fiona," he said to Alanna as she walked into the kitchen. "She's already at the schoolhouse with Brodie starting to rehearse."

"No one can resist the Reverend Dunn for long," Aileen said, sliding a full plate toward Alanna. "I'm headed to rehearsals too."

"What's your part?" Alanna asked her.

"Townsperson Number Nine," Aileen said proudly. "We can always use more people in the crowd scenes. Shall the two of you come with me, then?"

"Why not?" Joe said. "This is the most incredible jam I've ever had by the way, Aileen. It's like the berries just came out of the field."

Well, this was a switch. He was all smiles toward his hostess and willing to take a part in *Brigadoon*. Evidently a big breakfast had the ability to wipe out all of Joe's doubts about Alloway, Alanna thought, as she put a cloth napkin across her lap and accepted Aileen's offer of crumpets.

Aileen gave them a huge smile in return. "Did you two sleep well, or were you crowded?" she asked. "Such a nice young couple you are, so clearly well matched. I do hope you managed in such a small bed."

Alanna shot Joe a stern look, but he was happily stuffing the last bit of food in his mouth.

"All done," he announced, wiping his mouth. "I could eat that jam all day long."

"I'll give you a jar for the road, then," Aileen held one out. She was all smiles. Seemed like she enjoyed having a houseful again, and Alanna thought what a wonderful mother she must have been to these boys. Then it occurred to her that perhaps both Brodie and Colin hadn't always lived in the same house. *Well,* she thought, *all the answers will come to me one day.*

At Dunn's insistence, Emma had slipped off to the wings and then returned in the red dress, which was clearly too long for her. Actually, too big overall. She made a tentative turn and the dress flopped around her legs.

"See," she said, swirling around. "It doesn't fit. That's got to be a sign."

Alanna, Joe, and Aileen were entering just in time to hear the last line. "I can help alter it," Alanna heard herself calling out.

"Do you even know how to sew?" Joe asked quietly.

"Evidently," she whispered back. And then, speaking louder toward the frowning Emma and the smiling Dunn,

"It only needs to be hemmed and perhaps run a seam up the back."

"And Skye can help you," Dunn said. "She's quite handy with a needle."

"I can't ask her to alter the dress when I'm the reason she's not wearing it," Emma said. "She's got to be angry with me."

"Nonsense, child, Skye sees what we all do, that your presence here is a godsend," Dunn said. "This kind lady can take the dress to her house, and you can stay here and begin practicing your lines with Brodie. Here he is now."

Brodie approached the stage as if he were walking toward a firing squad instead of a rehearsal.

Emma looked at him as he climbed onto the stage and said, "It looks as if *Brigadoon* has the wrong Fiona and the wrong Tommy as well," she said. "But shall we make the best of it?"

Brodie nodded, with his usual taciturn manner. "We can start with the ballet. It's the toughest part."

"It is," Emma said. "But my favorite scene, as well."

Alanna scrambled up to take the red dress from Dunn who crossed the stage and seated himself at an old piano.

"You enter stage left, dear," he said to Emma. "Remember?"

"Yes," Emma said quietly, moving stage left. "It's all coming back to me in pieces. I even think I dreamed about it."

Joe slid down in his seat. *Give me a courtroom drama any day over this*, he thought. *Broken hearts, broken legs, dresses that don't fit, a stand-in cousin with an attitude.* But evidently the show would go on no matter what.

NINE

Of all the cute things in Alloway, Alanna thought, Skye's cottage had to be the cutest. She'd followed the ridiculously easy directions she'd been given by Reverend Dunn—to the small house at the end of one of the village's three paths leading from the one main street—and pushed open the gate. She imagined that, in the spring, the small yard would be full of flowers. At this time of year, snow drifts covered the bird bath and benches, creating soft sculptures that melted into the cushioned garden.

She knocked on the green wooden door. A pause, then a voice from within.

"Come in."

Evidently, locked doors weren't an issue in the village, but still. Skye was expecting a neighbor or relative to enter. Not a woman claiming to be Emma's friend from America and bearing the red dress that Skye would no longer be wearing.

Alanna cautiously pushed open the door and was greeted by the fattest gray cat she'd ever seen, followed by the second fattest grey cat she'd ever seen. A fire crackled in the hearth, and the table was piled with dishes and pots. Yesterday's covered dish supper had been interrupted by Skye's fall and the subsequent dash to the clinic in Ayr, and all the food that had been prepared for the community meal had evidently made its way to Skye's table.

The last thing in the room Alanna's eyes fell on was Skye herself, propped up on a small settee with an afghan draped over the cast on her leg. She looked at Alanna curiously but didn't seem alarmed by the presence of a stranger in her sitting room.

Alanna spilled out the story of why she'd come, and Skye nodded briskly and reached for the dress. "So you sew too, you say?"

"A little," Alanna said, for she really wasn't at all sure if she did. One of the more interesting things about having so little recall of your life is that you were constantly surprising yourself with unexpected skills and scraps of stray knowledge.

"We were thinking we'd just baste it up a little," she went on, as Skye spread the full red skirt across her lap. "Because you'll be taking the role back next year, of course."

"We'll need to do more than baste," Skye said matter-of-factly. Apparently, she truly did hold no malice toward Emma or even any regret over missing her annual chance to shine in the village play. "The dancing is more vigorous than one might guess, and we canna have the dress coming apart on her halfway through the ballet. We must take it apart at the waist and, if you can hem it, I'll work on the top half. The sooner we get it fitted to Emma, the better."

Skye told Alanna where to find her sewing kit, and the two set to work. Alanna shooed one of the cats off the rocking chair and pulled it closer to the settee where Skye was already clipping threads.

"You're being very kind about this whole thing," Alanna said. "Does your leg hurt much?"

"Ahh, the pain killers do precisely what they promise," Skye said with a laugh. "But I fear my senses are being killed along with the pain. Stop me if I start to sew the neck together or cut the sleeves off."

"Brodie is helping Emma rehearse until Colin returns," Alanna ventured. She didn't want to keep probing a painful subject, but she was curious about Skye's relationship with Colin. So far, she and Joe hadn't done much Wish Granting, and she was beginning to suspect that their task wasn't so much about reuniting Colin and Emma as it was about handling the hurt feelings and disappointment that might come with such a reunion.

"He knows the part well."

"Well enough to cover if Colin doesn't make it back in time?"

Skye glanced at her curiously. "I suppose. But there's no reason to expect it will come to that. Come what may, Colin manages to make it back to Alloway every new year, doesn't he?"

That strange British custom, Alanna thought, of ending a sentence with a question.

Skye had clipped the threads holding the bottom of the dress from the top and she slid the skirt over to Alanna, wincing a little as she moved. "How many centimeters must we raise the skirt?"

"Centimeters? Oh dear, I'm not sure. Emma is five four."

Skye frowned.

"Five feet, four inches tall," Alanna amended. "And you're ... I'd guess more like my height, five seven, so that's three inches, which is ..." She trailed off in dismay. Why hadn't she paid more attention when they learned the metric system in school?

"Take the skirt up about 8 centimeters," Skye said, handing her a tape measure. "We don't want her to trip while they're doing the ballet. And Colin will be back in time, no matter what. Eight years and he's never missed a performance."

"Has anyone called him? Told him of your accident and his new Fiona?"

"I don't know. His time with his daughter is very limited, you see. Very precious. She's a love of a thing."

"What do you think are the odds of him winning custody?" Alanna knew she was hovering on the verge of rudeness by asking so many personal questions, but she felt she had to know. "Is his wife really as heartless as Aileen implied?"

Skye laughed. "No, I wouldn't say Destiny was heartless. Alloway was never her cup of tea, try as she might, but there's no sin in that. This sort of life isn't for everyone."

"Her name's Destiny?"

"Oh, you haven't heard the worst of it. Destiny Bane is the whole name. Her parents were hippies, I believe was the story."

"Jesus. No wonder she wanted to get married."

Skye nodded agreeably. "You would think so, wouldn't you? But she came to us as 'Ms. Bane' and left the same way."

"Oh, so she kept her maiden name. Curious. Is that one of the reasons she's disliked around town? I take it the citizens of Alloway, especially the older ladies, are rather traditional."

Skye frowned, peering at the seams as she sewed. "The problem is that some of the people in town, especially those Aileen's age, behave as if Alloway really is

Brigadoon, and the whole town will simply cease to exist if anyone leaves. Especially Colin. He's rather the pet of the village, you see, so they've all been much harder on Destiny than the situation warranted."

Now that, Alanna thought, was an interesting speech for several reasons. When Emma had recalled Colin's time in the States, she had said that the family he stayed with treated him like a pet, and here Skye was using exactly the same phrase to describe him. It made it sound like Colin was stuck in time, more boy than man, and perhaps too charming for anyone to take him seriously. And it was also strange that Skye of all people would come to the defense of Destiny Bane, the woman Colin had chosen over her. Perhaps Brodie was wrong when he claimed Skye had been in love with Colin for years, since she was not only sympathetic toward his wife, but she was now coming to the aid of this latest interloper as well. Ripping out the seams of her own costume for Emma, a woman who had taken her part in the play and would dearly love to take her leading man. The girl was either amazingly tolerant or a fool. But, Alanna reasoned, perhaps she didn't really understand all the undercurrents of Alloway.

Alanna had finished taking out the hem and gave the skirt a shake. "I would think Colin would be willing to follow his wife and child to London. Alloway doesn't seem like his cup of tea either."

Skye laughed, a gentle sound. "We're all surprised by his sudden loyalty. For all his prattle about starting over in some grand new place, it turns out Colin has become a bit of a homebody. Doesn't really want to raise a child in the city."

"You know his daughter?"

92

"Of course. When she was here last summer, I kept her while he and Brodie worked the fields. Emma and I had a grand time. We'd pack a lunch each day and take ..."

Wait a minute. This gets stranger and stranger, Alanna thought. "His daughter is named Emma?"

"He always said it was his favorite name," Skye said quietly. "Now I suppose I know why. Anyway, that's what Colin calls her as a pet name. And what we all call her when she's in Alloway."

At last Skye's guard was down for, when she looked at Alanna, her face said it all. Skye really did love Colin, and she was no fool. She knew precisely what Emma's sudden arrival meant—and that look said it was eating her up inside.

Alanna pretended to focus on her work, but she was really wondering what it all meant. She could practically hear Joe whispering in her ear, "What it means is that this case has gotten more complicated yet again. What it means is that we'll be stuck in MacHootersville until Easter."

The two women fell into silence, each focused on her needle and thread.

So she's waited here patiently, Alanna thought, somehow sure that the day would come when Colin would come back to Alloway. Colin goes off to travel the world and Skye waits. He marries the London girl and Skye waits. And now, just when he seems on the verge of recognizing how wonderful his hometown had been all along, just on the verge of returning to the local girl who had loved him for years ... Emma from America shows up.

Alanna shook her head, struggling to keep her mind on her sewing and on who their client was. She and Joe were here to help Emma, not Skye. It wasn't their job to make life fair. Still, she felt torn. This sweet girl should have her chance, too.

"Do you resent me?" she asked.

He was looking up at her. His breath was in her face. In fact, his breath was as close as her own. She could see everything from this angle, lifted above him in his arms, her hands resting on his shoulders. Resting lightly. There was no need to dig in and grab. He had her. She was safe.

His scent was all around them—sweet hay and soap, and mist. A hundred different kinds of cleanliness, of wholesomeness. She felt light in his arms and, before she realized it, she was glad he was the one holding her, lifting her above the stage where she felt suddenly, fleetingly, an overwhelming sense of happiness.

"Why should I resent you, lass?" he asked, but his voice did not sound harsh, but rather surprised.

She started to say, "Because I'm not what you expected," and then stopped herself. He wasn't what she'd expected either. She'd expected Colin. She could say that he resented her because she'd shown up out of nowhere, moved into his house, forced him into a week of rehearsals, usurped the lead in his village play.

But that wasn't it either. If he resented her, it was because she was doing something to him, evoking changes in him that were beyond his will.

She knew this because that's *why* she was starting to resent *him*. It had begun with the communion cup and, today, as Dunn directed them through the steps of the dance, it was getting worse. He was confusing her. Making her doubt herself. Making her start to forget why she'd come to Alloway in the first place. And she remembered how he had made Alanna laugh and recited poetry. That was a different Brodie. Not the stolid, monosyllabic Brodie he had shown to Emma.

Emma remained motionless in the pose but mentally shook her head. She was making the exact same stupid mistake she'd made ten years ago, imagining that a musical could come to life. This was nothing. A rehearsal. They were dancing. Planned steps, with a planned lift at the end. Brodie had no problem raising her up at arm's length above his head. Holding her there while Dunn shouted out directions about the lighting, focused everything on the two of them. This was Fiona and Tommy's big moment, after all. The scene in which they kiss.

Joe would say that ballet is boring. An effete dance aimed at intellectuals—the physical equivalent of an epic poem. But the truth is different. It's physical, earthy, and sensual. It makes the dancers sweat, grow breathless, tremble with the effort of holding absolutely still. When the two of them were in this lift, the length of their bodies pressed against each other, close enough that Emma could hear Brodie's breathing, smell the fresh scent of his hair, feel the pounding of his heart against her thigh, she realized that her memory had excluded these sensations and focused only on the kiss. But she and Colin had done more than kiss so long ago. They had shared this pure physical excitement.

"I have a role," Joe said proudly when Alanna returned, carrying the altered version of the red dress.

"Townsperson Number Ten?"

"Please. Dunn could tell at a glance that I was meant for bigger things. At the very end of the play, when Tommy returns to Brigadoon and kisses Fiona, the church bell is supposed to ring. Twelve times. Midnight, get it?"

"I get it. The end of the day and the moment where Brigadoon goes to sleep for another hundred years."

Joe beamed. "Dunn wants me to be the one to ring the bell."

"Congratulations," Alanna said, sinking to the chair beside him. "But we've got more complications."

"I'll say. Brodie and Emma ... they dance really great together."

"What's wrong with that? It's good she's picking the routines up quickly, isn't it? That's certainly what everyone's counting on."

Joe smirked. "I think she's picking up a whole lot more than the routines. They've got chemistry, she and Brodie. Even Dunn saw it. They've got the kind of chemistry a minister can see."

"So what are you saying? Now she's interested in Brodie?"

Joe leaned back in his chair and gazed thoughtfully at the empty stage. "Who knows? Maybe. Women seem to be a lot slower than men in this particular area. Everyone's taken a break for lunch and you can see them together yourself this afternoon. What did you mean by 'complications'?"

"Skye ... she doesn't just have a thing for Colin; she loves his little girl, too. When I started looking around, I saw pictures of the child all over the house, including a picture of Colin and Skye and the little girl standing on the bridge, all smiling like crazy and looking like the perfect family. Oh, and here's the good part: the wife is named Destiny Bane."

"Who the hell would go to a lawyer named Destiny Bane?"

"No one, I'd imagine, and yet she doesn't grab the chance to dump the name and become Destiny MacGregor. It gets better. What do you think Colin wanted to name his little girl?"

"Fiona?"

"Close. Emma. He told Skye it was his favorite name. But Destiny nixed it and named the baby Chance. What on Earth do you think that means?"

Joe frowned and then, lawyer-like, began ticking off the possibilities, using a different finger for each one. "Well, it could mean that Colin carried a flame for Emma all these many years, just as she carried one for him. It could mean he likes the name because it reminds him of his time in America, where evidently everyone treated him like a star. Or it could mean absolutely nothing. But wait a minute; I don't like where this is going. So what if they looked like a family in that picture? It's not your job to get Skye together with Colin. Anyway, the wife got her way, didn't she, naming the baby Chance?"

"Just like it's not your job to get Emma together with Brodie."

"Point taken. We've just got to grant Emma's wish, which was nothing more than to see Colin again, and from there, the chips fall where they may."

"Quick in and out, isn't that what you said? A slam dunk of a case and then you're on to the next?" *And just a little bit closer to being back on Earth for good,* she thought.

Back to your law practice and women who don't dissolve when you try to kiss them. Women you wouldn't hesitate a second to take to bed, not even if God himself warned you not to.

Joe nodded. "Quite right. We're not here to engineer some sort of fairy tale, even if the setting is right for one."

"I thought you said this was a boring little town halfway to nowhere," Alanna said. "I thought you wanted to get out of here as fast as you could."

"So maybe I'm falling under the spell of Brigadoon just a wee bit," Joe said, suddenly popping to his feet. "Do you know what we need? We need a little chit-chat with Morgan."

TEN

Dunn presented like the quintessential kindly village pastor, but, as a theatrical director, he was a stern taskmaster—demanding that Emma and Brodie go through the ballet time and time again. Especially the part, near the opening, where Emma as Fiona runs lightly across the stage and makes a small leap into Brodie-as-Tommy's arms.

It's the kind of move that, if done correctly, may look effortless, which is the goal, but in reality the dance lift required a precise sort of timing, a wordless communication between the woman who leaps and the man who catches her. Emma and Brodie had practiced that one move over and over until the church bells struck noon, and finally Brodie had turned to Dunn with Emma in his arms, and said, "Gad, man, do you plan to kill us?"

So Dunn had finally relented and sent everyone home for an hour, just enough time to eat lunch and rest up for more rehearsals.

Emma knew she should take advantage of the break to find some lunch, but she wasn't sure quite how to do that. There were no chain restaurants in Alloway, and she knew of no pub or café that was open. Going back to ask Aunt Aileen to serve another meal seemed like an imposition, but it appeared to be her only option, so off she went back to Aileen's cottage. But when she got there, Emma found the kitchen deserted, herself the only one in the house. She thought it would be presumptuous to dig through the pantry and fridge looking for food, so Emma stood for a moment in the empty kitchen, uncertain what to do next.

It was the first time that the limitations of Alloway had really struck her. Yes, it is indeed a wonderful thing to eat with your family, to slow down and really take a leisurely meal. But was it a wonderful thing to do it three times a day, or if a home-cooked meal was your only option? What happened if you only had a few minutes for lunch?

But that was probably a nonsense question. No one in the village appeared to ever be in a hurry.

Resigned to her solitude, Emma walked up the narrow staircase to Colin's room—her room for the time being. She pushed the door open and sniffed the air. Perhaps it was just her imagination, but it seemed that, even in the past twenty-four hours, the masculine scent had dissipated a bit, almost as if Colin's presence was seeping from the room little by little every hour she occupied it.

But still ... his clothes, his pictures, his books surrounded her. Emma stretched across the bed and realized, the minute her muscles relaxed, that she was not only hungry but physically tired as well. To perform the dance, she should have been exercising those muscles for weeks beforehand, and she wondered whether Skye had prepared herself for the rigors of the performance.

Emma rolled onto her back and looked up at the ceiling. If she was tired, Brodie must be completely exhausted. Although Emma weighed no more today than she had on that fall morning ten years ago when she had first auditioned for the part. But to catch and lift anyone—even a dancer who weighed no more than Emma—so many times as they had that morning would take a toll on a man, and Brodie had been extraordinarily careful with her. Each time they went into the lift, she could feel his left arm close immediately around her, his right arm firmly supporting her thighs.

"I've got you," he said once, roughly, as he seemed to say everything. But she knew it was true.

Dunn's plan was that she would leap, Brodie would catch her, and then he would spin her in a series of circles diagonally across the stage, while her head lolled back and her eyes closed. "Lost in the moment, you see, lass," he'd said, and she did see. It was exactly right, exactly what the character of Fiona would be. And Brodie was a farmer, a working man who routinely lifted and carried things much heavier than Emma. A man she could certainly count on to catch her. But to lie back in his arms like that required a pure raw vulnerability, and closing her eyes while he twirled them across the stage was dizzying. Once she had jerked to attention in the middle of a spin, her body startling like a sleeping baby's, and when she'd opened her eyes she had been momentarily disoriented. Where was she? What year was this? What man was with her? Was she truly Fiona or still just Emma?

It was getting harder and harder to distinguish reality from fantasy, Emma thought, pulling the quilt over her hips and letting her eyes close. The dance and the music were enough to transport her straight back to tenth grade, to the moment when she had closed her arms around Colin's neck and drawn her face close to his. But Colin was taller than Brodie, more slender, and he had been merely sixteen. Back then the director had not suggested that he spin across the stage with Emma in his arms, had not ordered her to lean precipitously back, testing their balance even further. Back then, Emma had held herself upright in Colin's trembling arms, extending her foot to find the floor as soon as possible, to help him set her down gently, not plop her to the ground with a relieved thud. And she had most certainly kept her eyes open the whole time.

Emma was not quite correct when she'd concluded that there was no place to get a quick lunch in Alloway. There was one small pub in town, but it had no sign, no menu posted in the window, no chalkboard out front listing the specials. You either knew to go there or you didn't, and Morgan did. He waved to Joe and Alanna through the front window as they passed. They froze in their tracks, looked at each other and shrugged, and then entered the restaurant and joined him. None of their three chairs matched, Alanna noticed, and the table had a most definite wobble. But within seconds a woman lumbered from the kitchen bearing three large steins of dark bitter ale. Apparently in Alloway, happy hour started just after noon.

"Thanks for signaling to us," Alanna said, while Joe lit into the ale. "We weren't sure where we were headed or even if you were still in town."

Morgan smiled, showing even white teeth. "Not an imposition. I'm taking Skye back to the doctor this afternoon for a check on her leg, poor lamb."

"Poor lamb? You do realize you're starting to speak Scottish too," Joe said. "Less than two days in town and this morning I heard myself referring to something as 'a wee bit of bother.'"

Morgan laughed. "'Tis a charming language, is it not?"

102

But Alanna was ready to get right to the point. "I'm glad you mentioned Skye. What if she has a wish too?"

"She undoubtedly does," Morgan said, dropping the brogue. "Everyone has a wish."

"What I mean is ... can we grant it?"

"We're not trying to tell you how to do your job," Joe broke in hastily. "It's just that we've observed certain things throughout the morning and were thinking ..."

"Skye loves Colin and she has her whole life," Alanna said. "Really loves him, and not just in a schoolgirl crush sort of way. She even loves his little girl. And then there's the fact that, at least according to Joe, Emma belongs with Brodie, although she doesn't know it yet. He's faithful and loyal and strong and all the things she really needs in a man. So we're thinking that, if there's some way we can just get Emma to stop fantasizing about Colin and really see what's in front of her, and get Colin to stop running around the world and really see what's in front of him ..."

"Ah," said Morgan. "Two days on the job and already you know what they all need better than they know themselves. If I recall, Emma's wish was to find her old love Colin, nothing more and nothing less."

"It's frustrating," Alanna said. "Watching people want all the wrong things."

Morgan took a drink of ale. "Tell me about it. I guess my questions to you would be, 'Why is this bothering you so much? And why are you taking this case so personally?'"

"It's not personal," Alanna said quickly. Too quickly. She pushed her hair back out of her face and looked around the room. A few other tables had filled. Everyone was drinking ale. And eating the same kind of stew, evidently. This little town, she thought. It's limited and insular, so why am I so drawn to it? Everything seems so simple on the surface, but then again everything is simple on the surface everywhere.

Joe tried to get the conversation back on track. "So what we're asking is ..."

Morgan cut Joe off with a glance. "What you're asking is if you can override Emma's wish and give her what the two of you have decided is what she really needs. You're asking if you can give Emma's wish to Skye. You're basically saying that, after two assignments, you already think you've outgrown the role of Wish Granter and consider yourselves completely ready to play God."

"And apparently playing God is your job," Alanna snapped. Joe looked at her warningly. What had gotten into his partner? She was usually the patient one, the polite one, the one who followed the rules. And now she was being rude to Morgan, almost entirely without provocation. Being all angry and weepy and weird. Did female Wish Granters still have periods?

"The answer to both your questions is 'No,'" Morgan said. "No, you can't give Emma's wish to Skye, and no, you can't wish something new on Emma's behalf. People must find their own routes. They must seize their own destinies. We can't force them into happy endings, and we can't tie their lives up in a neat little bow. That isn't what the wishes are about."

Alanna arched an eyebrow. "The wishes aren't meant to make people happy?"

"The wishes are to help them grow. And part of growth is realizing on your own when you've wasted enough time wishing for the wrong thing." He held up a warning finger. "A wish can be powerful, but it can also be limiting. All humans have wishes. Most more than one.

104

But people must come to their own conclusion in their own time. Remember our motto."

"We'll grant your wish, but what happens next is up to you," Joe said mechanically, but it resonated within him and made him think about it in a new way. "Emma wished to kiss Colin, and kiss Colin she shall." He knew he'd been getting off track and that it had been lucky that they had happened to pass Morgan, who was so undeniably good at getting Joe refocused. Finishing up this case and getting on to the next one, that was all that really mattered. Getting back to the chance to re-live his own life. And he'd damn sure do a better job of it this time than last. That much at least was certain. But the possibility that he might never get that chance was something he refused to consider.

Alanna remained unconvinced. "So you're telling us that none of these things we've observed really matter? You're telling us we can't influence the situation at all?"

Morgan drained his ale and stood up to leave, winking at Alanna as he dropped a handful of coins on the table. "Can't influence the situation? Now when did I say something crazy like that?"

ELEVEN

Talking to Morgan always made Alanna pensive, and today was no different. As Joe scurried back to the schoolhouse to resume his duties as an unofficial stagehand and bell ringer, she bundled up and went for a walk along the perimeter of the village. The hills beyond Alloway were so still that the only sign of movement was Morgan's cab, chugging slowly along the only road into and out of town, presumably taking Skye to her doctor's appointment.

Alanna knew they couldn't save everyone or grant every wish. That wasn't the job they'd been sent to do. But the injustice of Skye's position still bothered Alanna, and Morgan's words kept ringing in her ears. Why did it bother her so much?

Was there a time she had loved a man who didn't love her in return?

She didn't think so. She thought, in fact, that it was more of the opposite. That a man had wanted her and she hadn't wanted him.

Had she waited for a man who went away and didn't come back?

Closer. But still not entirely right.

Alanna's feet crunched in the ice as she walked. The shards of her memory seemed to turn up just when she least expected them. On their first case, in Las Vegas, she had deduced that her Earthly wealth had not been enough to make her happy. It had not been enough to hold Alanna and her fiancé together or to even keep her tied to the Earthly plane. What she had always craved, she saw

106

now, was the kind of quiet simplicity that a town like Alloway offered. Being tied to nature and the slow turn of the seasons. Making jam and hemming dresses. Knowing your neighbors. Loving the boy next door.

Alanna stopped at the bridge and leaned over the railing. It was the perfect place to stand alone and dream, she thought, and she wondered how often Colin had come here. Or Skye. Perhaps even Brodie.

Things kept coming back to her. She had often remembered the ocean, riding the waves in early morning, alone on a beach in Florida. She had been body-surfing on the day she'd been taken to Transition. She also had remembered an engagement ring and a man walking through a door, leaving her in anger, but she had never known how to reconcile all these images. Now, in just this moment, it was beginning to come together.

Her fiancé had been obsessed with power, success, status, and all that came with it. He wanted to live in a big city. She had not. That difference between them—so simple and yet so profound—is what had led to her pulling off the engagement ring, him walking out in anger. It was the reason she had been on that beach alone.

Earlier that morning she had thought she was like Brodie. But she was also very much like Skye. A woman who wanted a simple life, in love with a man who wanted the world. Alanna may have been swimming on a beach in Florida and Skye may be ensconced in a small Scottish village, but their stories were the same. They were the ones who stayed behind. Who waited and hoped that a man would love them enough to also love the place that held them in its palms and nurtured their souls. That was why she was so determined to help Skye. She wanted to give Skye the happy ending she had never gotten for herself.

"You know, when I first saw you, I thought you might actually be Colin," Emma was saying to Brodie. "But when you got closer, I realized ..."

"I was more like Colin with a gut?" Brodie said.

"You don't have a gut," Emma protested with a laugh. "You just have a more muscular build."

"Aye," he muttered. "Muscles come from working the fields, holding the horses, and living out here where there's no one but yourself to rely on."

"Well, all that's a good thing if you're going to lift me up and carry me all over the stage. It'll take someone who can stand on his own."

"But I'll not be, in the end, will I? Colin will be lifting and twirling you about."

Emma felt as if she'd been slapped. What an idiot she could be. Of course, Brodie was a stand-in for a man who would be returning in a couple of days. A man she had come to Scotland specifically to kiss.

She and Brodie were once again standing on an empty stage, but this time the whole room was empty. Dunn, Joe, and the other workers had gone up to the prop room to gather the last of the swords and kilts.

"We could go through the ballet again," Brodie said, conscious that she felt awkward. "Or we could take a break."

"Let's take a break," Emma said. "A walk. Was this your school?"

Brodie nodded. "For twelve straight years. Come, I'll give you the grand tour."

They walked down the hall connecting the auditorium to the classrooms. Every school in the world must smell exactly the same, Emma thought. Some eternal combination of chalk dust, linoleum floors, and children. The doors to the classrooms were closed but each one was festively decorated for Christmas. One room for two grades, she noted by the signs on the door. Alloway was a small village indeed.

"The lunchroom," Brodie said, pointing toward another classroom. "I'm afraid we don't have a glamorous American cafeteria. The children bring a packed lunch from home. Grades one through five eat at noon, then six through twelve thirty minutes after." Alanna glanced through the door. It could scarcely be more different from the lunchroom in the school where she taught. The academy had salad bars and food stations serving pizza, deli sandwiches, and sushi under glass, and the kids still complained there wasn't anything good to eat.

Brodie was watching her, a bemused smile on his face. "Where to next?"

"The gym?"

He chuckled. "Afraid you saw it on your way in. Our playground is our gymnasium. Swings and see saws and climbing bars. Did you miss the soccer fields?"

"I suppose I did, considering there are fields surrounding fields in Alloway," she said. "But what do the children do for exercise in the winter?"

"They use these marvelous things we've invented," he said, his brogue growing more outrageous, and she knew he was teasing her. He leaned in to whisper, so close that the afternoon growth of his beard scraped gently against her face. "We call them coats and hats."

"Of course," she said, laughing awkwardly. "The delicate little blossoms at my school would never agree to outdoor sports in winter. Although," she added, "to be fair, girls can be pretty competitive at times. And most of them *do* ski, and some ice skate. But that's different, isn't it?"

"I wouldn't compare where you teach to our little school. Different planets, I suspect. And here's our last stop," Brodie said. "The library."

He swung open the door and they walked into the hushed room. Each wall was lined with shelves, each shelf crammed full of books. A desk sat in the middle, a globe on one end, a dictionary on the other. It looked like a school library from a museum.

"A very notable absence," Brodie said. "We don't have computers. And no, before you say anything, the kids don't carry iPhones or laptops. A few of the families in the village have home computers and there's one for general use in the town hall. But our dream is to have three of them in the school library. It's one thing to send the children outside to play in coats and mittens. It's another to send them to college unable to use the Internet."

Emma turned to face him. "I don't know how the teachers have managed as long as they have. Does the town ..."

"Have a Starbucks with Wi-Fi?"

"No, that isn't what I was going to say at all. Does the town have a plan for making this dream come true?"

He looked at her archly. "I'm afraid you're it."

"You plan to hold me hostage until America sends you a bunch of laptops?" She said it with a laugh, but secretly Emma felt a flush of shame. There was so much waste back at her old school. They must have a hundred laptops, even though each student also had her own. Wait a minute? Had she just referred to the school where she currently taught as "her old school"? It was one of the best girls prep schools in the country. Over thirty percent of their graduates each year went on to Ivies or little Ivies. And she'd been thrilled to get that job.

"No, we'll release you back to your homeland promptly on New Year's Day," Brodie said. "But we plan to use the proceeds of this year's play to buy computers for the school."

"It's wonderful," Emma said, "to use the proceeds for that. And I admire you for using the word 'we' even when you don't have any children in the school. Half the time we can't get our students' parents to miss a business meeting or charity function to come to a teacher conference, and here the whole town rallies around the school."

"Well yes," Brodie said, "the town is committed to the school, but I used the word 'we' because I'm on the education council."

"You're a marvel," Emma said. "I really admire that."

Brodie shook his head. "Only went to the local college myself, you know."

"What difference does that make?"

"I never got to go to America, you see. Only London a few times. My life has been tied to Alloway and the farm and the people here.

"Anyway, the words of the play seem to be coming back to you awfully fast," he said. "Everyone is talking among themselves, whispering that Emma must be a very clever lass indeed."

Emma walked over to the desk and spun the globe. The world blurred and she held a fingertip to the spinning orb, wondering where it would stop. It was a game she had played with her father, years ago. He used to tell her that wherever her finger was, when the globe stopped spinning, was where she would live when she grew up. She smiled faintly. How long had it been since she had played the globe game? In the age of MapQuest, globes seemed rather quaint. As did the portrait of Robert Burns on the wall in front of her.

"I'm not that clever," she told Brodie. "I may have a formal education, but I'm beginning to think I've been rather foolish in my life. That I have a very definite tendency to confuse fantasy with reality." She exhaled and raised her eyes to meet his. "Like, for example, imagining that I truly am the character I happen to be playing, taking certain things too much to heart."

"Perhaps," Brodie said, "we're our most true selves when we are pretending. Perhaps playing a role gives us the courage to say and do the things we would fear to do otherwise."

Emma pulled her finger away from the globe. It was still spinning. "Perhaps," she said, but it came out more like a whisper. And then she asked, "Do the children know how great a poet their village gave the world?" She glanced up at the old portrait of Burns with his dark eyebrows, wavy hair, the white shirt close around his neck, almost reaching his jawline. Could a portrait ever capture the poet's longings, his wishes?

Brodie came over to her side and, with no warning, began to recite.

Ae fond kiss, and then we sever;
Ae fareweel, and then forever!
Deep in heart-wrung tears I'll pledge thee,
Warring sighs and groans I'll wage thee.
Who shall say that Fortune grieves him,
While the star of hope she leaves him?
Me, nae cheerfu' twinkle lights me;
Dark despair around benights me.

I'll ne'er blame my partial fancy,
Naething could resist my Nancy;
But to see her was to love her;
Love but her, and love forever.
Had we never lov'd sae kindly,
Had we never lov'd sae blindly,
Never met—or never parted—
We had ne'er been broken-hearted.

Fare thee weel, thou first and fairest!
Fare thee weel, thou best and dearest!
Thine be ilka joy and treasure,
Peace. Enjoyment, love, and pleasure!
Ae fond kiss, and then we sever;
Ae fareweel, alas, forever!
Deep in heart-wrung tears I'll pledge thee,
Warring sighs and groans I'll wage thee!

Emma listened to the words—recited, she thought, as
they always should be, by someone whose native tongue
was that of the poet—and, as Brodie finished, she looked

up at the portrait again and then at Brodie, really seeing him for the first time.

"Aye," he said softly, that gruff tone gone, at least for the moment, "I think the children understand the value of their village poet and learn more than a few of his poems over the years. As I did.

"Come on then," he said and reached for her hand. "Time to get back to rehearsal. Perhaps if Fiona and Tommy dance a thousand more times, Dunn will finally be satisfied."

TWELVE

Joe said, "We need two things. First, what we need is a storm. A huge airport-closing storm. The kind that shuts down cities and strands people for days."

"And we need that because?" asked Alanna.

"To keep Colin in London over New Year's. If Brodie plays opposite Emma in the play, it will give her more time to see he's the right guy."

"Listen to yourself. Half the time all you want to do is grant the original wish and half the time you're plotting to change everything. You heard Morgan. We can fine-tune things here and there, but we can't change the course of history. Besides, do we know for a fact that Brodie's the right guy? Neither of us have ever even seen Colin."

Joe sputtered. "Colin's a lightweight. Brodie's the guy."

"Okay, for the sake of argument, let's say he is. How exactly are you and I supposed to produce a storm strong enough to close Gatwick Airport?"

"I don't quite have that part figured out yet."

"What else do we need?"

"A villain. Everybody on this case is just too damn nice."

Emma laughed and got to her feet. It was their fourth morning in Alloway. She and Joe had just finished another one of Aileen's gargantuan breakfasts and were alone in the house. "What makes you think Brodie even wants to play Tommy?" she asked, picking up her plate and heading toward the sink.

"You know Tommy's big song? 'It's Almost Like Being in Love'?"

Alanna shook her head. "Maybe this is the wrong time to confess this to a man who's hell-bent on being Dunn's assistant, but I don't know this play. And I haven't spent all day in rehearsals like you have. You know that Skye and I have been swamped with the costumes. Bring me your plate and cup and I'll wash everything up."

"It's almost like we've settled into a nice pastoral routine here. Me eating a hearty breakfast before going out to wrestle the plow, you clearing away breakfast before you do the mending."

"Would you rather take on the dishes? I'll gladly relinquish that chore." But as she said it, Alanna realized that—standing here at the sink in front of a little window that looked out onto rolling fields covered in snow—she felt peace and even, yes, joy.

"No, seriously. I doubt Aileen expects us to wash up. We're paying guests, after all. And besides, can't you do sort of a *Bewitched* thing: Twitch your nose and clean a whole house?"

"Yeah, right, being a Wish Granter is just like being a TV witch. I sort of like puttering around the house. Doing dishes, making beds ... and now that I've got the hang of it, I'm even enjoying helping Skye sew. I wonder what that means?"

Joe grinned at her. "It means that on Earth you were rich enough to have servants and therefore you find simple domestic tasks to be exotic. Because, trust me, if you'd been a wife and mother on Earth, the thrill of washing dishes would have worn off pretty fast."

116

Alanna turned back toward the sink. Joe teased her a lot, but something in his banter today was getting beneath her skin. He knew she didn't like being reduced to the role of poor little rich girl, and that her wealth had been the source of as many problems as pleasures in her life. So it was bad enough that he was joking about her being rich, but then he also dragged in the bit about how she hadn't been a wife or mother. He knew these were hardly laughing matters to her, and yet ...

There was something else, too: something Alanna hardly admitted to herself. Joe was still keeping his distance. The last three nights had been a repeat of the first. They had told everyone goodnight, climbed the stairs, entered the bedroom, and he had disappeared. Sometime over the course of their time in Scotland, Joe had evidently mastered the skill of disappearing when he wanted to—something she was still working on, without much success. And he was demonstrating his new ability at precisely ten every night.

It was one thing for him to follow Morgan's orders about keeping their distance. It was another thing that it was apparently so easy for him.

Almost as if avoiding her was a relief—or perhaps that was a thought that only she had, one for which there was no tangible evidence.

As Alanna wiped down the counter, Joe reached to pour himself another cup of tea. *We're a bit like an old married couple already*, Alanna thought. *He's ignoring me, almost as if he were reading the Dow Jones numbers, and I'm sulking. And that isn't good for our partnership no matter how you slice it.* What to do about it was perplexing.

"You never told me why you think Brodie wants to be in the play," she said, consciously making her voice light and friendly.

"Oh yeah, that song," Joe said. "It's called 'It's Almost Like Being in Love,' and it's Tommy's big moment, you know: the point where he confesses his feelings for Fiona. And Brodie was singing it this morning in the shower."

"Maybe he was just practicing," Alanna said.

"Why bother practicing if he's just the stand-in?"

"A lot of people sing in the shower."

"It's not an easy thing to be constantly overshadowed," Joe said. "I'm surprised Brodie hasn't run Colin through with a pitchfork by now."

"You're really making a lot of assumptions about their relationship," Alanna said. All the food was put away and the dishes were washed, and she too poured herself a final cup of tea. "Everyone says they're as close as brothers and that Brodie wanted to stay behind and take care of the family farm. So why are you so convinced he harbors all this jealousy toward Colin? Come to think of it, why are you so convinced Colin is a jerk?"

"I've known guys like that before," Joe said, pushing to his feet. "Come on, we need to get moving."

"I'm going to finish my tay," Alanna said, mimicking the accent she'd heard. "I'll see you later."

Joe looked down at her curiously. "Are you okay?"

"Sure. I just have some thinking to do."

"Seems like you've been thinking an awful lot lately."

Alanna shrugged. "What else is there to do in Alloway?"

Joe bundled up for the short walk to the school. Coat, hat, gloves, muffler. With a final glance back at Alanna, who was sipping her tea and staring thoughtfully into space, he pushed open the heavy wooden door and stepped into the street...

... where he was almost run down by a taxi-cab.

"Damn," he yelped, leaping back onto the sidewalk, just in time to avoid a double-decker red bus which hit its horn with a rude, startling sound. His shoe landed square in a nice big pile of dog doo and he brushed against a passing teenager who looked over his shoulder and cursed him.

Great. Just great. Traffic and noise and crowds and shit. Somehow he'd manifested himself back to London. Or had he really done that all by himself?

THIRTEEN

He may have been a rookie Wish Granter, but Joe had learned a few things about manifesting against his will. He knew that Morgan was usually behind it and that he usually had a very limited amount of time in the new place before he would be pulled out of it as abruptly as he'd been thrust into it. Involuntary manifestation was a bit like coming into a movie that had already started. You had to work very hard to bring yourself up to speed on the story, to figure out what must have happened just before you arrived. So Joe knew he would have to be more observant than usual in the minutes or hours to come.

Another thing. These abrupt transitions from one place to another were hard on the Wish Granters—leaving them weak, dizzy, and exhausted, as if their time in Transition was coming to a close and whatever life force was left to them was in peril. Morgan knew this, so he used the manifestations judiciously, only moving Alanna or Joe when they were either in emotional crisis or about to make a mistake. Joe hadn't been the least upset at the breakfast table, so he could only assume that he had been once again on the verge of some dramatic and stupid gesture.

What had he and Alanna been discussing? Oh yeah–Colin and Brodie. How Brodie was a stand-up guy, loyal and reliable, and Colin was just some sort of flake. And then boom, Joe is in London, where Colin is, and he could only assume he'd been sent there to observe Colin and get a sense of the broader picture.

The problem was, he had no idea where Colin MacGregor might be. London was a huge city, and he seemed to have manifested on some random crowded street.

Think, Joe; think. You've got a single father spending his last couple of vacation days with his toddler-aged daughter. Where might they go? It was awfully cold for an outing to the park. Would a child that age like the circus? Would she be old enough for a movie? Did they have things like Chuck E Cheese in England?

"Excuse me," Joe said to a passing woman. She was the perfect person to ask for advice: a seemingly pleasant and prosperous sort, with a small child at her side and another in a stroller. "But do you know where I might go if I wanted to find a little girl?"

The woman looked at him blankly.

"I'm just looking for the sort of place where lots of small children hang around," Joe said.

The woman made a startled noise, grabbed the hand of her own daughter more tightly, and rattled off down the street. Great. He was An American Pervert in London.

Okay, Joe; keep thinking. What's in London? Buckingham Palace. The British Museum. The Tower of London. The Globe Theater. Harrods.

Harrods. There's an idea. Even a childless man from America knew they had a huge toy department, a tearoom full of cakes and cookies. Colin had undoubtedly spoiled his daughter over Christmas, as divorced fathers always do. Presents and presents and more presents. But who knows? On the eve of his departure, he may have decided to let her select one final gift.

"These costumes have needed repair for years," Skye was saying. "But we really never had anyone truly devoted to the task." Her leg was still in a cast, but she was obviously feeling much better judging by the enthusiastic way she shook out a huge kilt that some local man would be wearing in the big bagpipe scene. "It's a blessing, really, that you're here and that I suddenly have enough time..."

"A blessing? You amaze me, Skye. You've been knocked off a ladder, have broken your leg, are unable to play the role you've taken for years—a role that everyone says you were wonderful in, by the way—and you call it all a blessing."

Skye flushed. "I imagine that I sound rather foolish to an American woman like yourself. Someone who has an important job ... what exactly do you do, anyway?"

Alanna winced. She always hated these moments. She wasn't a good liar. "I help people get where they're going."

Skye frowned. "Like a travel agent?"

"Yes, a travel agent."

"Well don't tell the Reverend Dunn or he'll catch hold of your sleeve and never turn loose. He's always looking for ways to promote the play, bring in more income, spread our local fame a bit farther."

It was Alanna's turn to frown. "How big can the production get? You only have the schoolhouse stage and the local actors ... and there isn't a hotel to accommodate visitors, even if you managed to bring them here. There are only a certain number of seats in the auditorium and a certain number of beds for lease in the village homes."

Skye smiled and pulled a stray thread from the kilt. "If you said all that to the reverend, I believe he would tell you that those circumstances are open to change."

122

"In a way, I'd hate to see it," Alanna said. She felt a bit agitated, although she wasn't sure why. It wasn't her town or her play or any of her business, really. But there was something so authentic about this homespun production that she recoiled from the thought of it becoming bigger. Floodlights instead of candles. Outside actors coming in from London. Sound systems instead of bagpipes on stage. A hotel with a coffee shop instead of Aileen's snug little kitchen. But no, if they built a hotel, they'd have to find ways to fill it year-round, wouldn't they? Festivals and fairs and more productions. Shuttle buses from Edinburgh instead of the occasional cab.

Alloway would become just another tourist trap.

"It's charming just as it is," she said, more calmly.

"Charming, aye," Skye agreed, and was it Alanna's imagination or did her voice sound slightly bitter? "But our little town is dying. We aren't the real Brigadoon, which only appears once in a hundred years. We have to find a way to keep going day after day. Our young people leave and never come back. Farming doesn't suit everyone, you know. And even if it did ..." She finished with the hemming and tossed the kilt aside. "The small family farm is dying, too," she finally said. "Just as it is in America, I'd imagine."

"So the solution is to make the play bigger?"

"I'm not sure there is any one solution, but I suppose bringing in more tourism money would be a start. I don't really know what the reverend envisions, but I imagine it involves a whole theater and a place where we could do year-round productions, not just at holidays when the school is out of session." She eyed the pile of plaid at her feet.

"That's all of them, and I thank you for your help. Do you mind taking them to the school?"

"Of course not," Alanna said, getting to her feet.

Skye shook her finger at her with mock severity. "And don't let Dunn hear you're a travel agent or he'll talk your ear off with his plans. Lots of Americans getting off a bus, dollars spilling from their pockets with every step. That's his dream."

Better be prepared for the spilling of Chinese yuan, Alanna thought, and laughed, but her heart wasn't in it. *It's not just Skye. This whole town needs a wish.*

FOURTEEN

The wind rushed down the street with enough force that Joe wondered if a major storm really was kicking up. It practically blew him into the doorman in front of the entrance to Harrods. Once inside, he looked around at this poshest of places. The high ceilings, piped-in classical music, and calm dignity of the iconic store impressed even the "rather more than a little world-weary" Joe. He paused to take in the framed portraits of Princess Diana and Dodi Al Fayed, the son of the Harrods owner, which were prominently displayed, as if their spirits were somehow being evoked to hover over the enterprise. Beyond them, not quite so prominently, was a portrait of the royal family. And standing next to them, was that ... yes it was, Morgan, with a big grin lighting up his face.

"Get down here," Joe hissed at the portrait. "I swear, you get more outrageous every day."

Morgan was suddenly beside him, snorting with pleasure over his little joke. He did seem to be amused by—well, by practically everything, now that Joe considered it. He'd never met anyone who laughed quite as easily, although his old law partner Russ had come close.

"Sorry," Morgan said. "Couldn't resist the chance to stand beside the Queen."

"I swear I don't know how you got this job. Weren't there others up there in Transition better qualified? At least more serious about it."

Morgan shrugged. "So sorry you don't approve of my managerial style. Follow me."

The last two words were a mere formality because Joe had no choice but to follow. He and Morgan dematerialized. Joe's previous involuntary manifests had been abrupt, nerve-wracking events, often accompanied by the sensation of being sucked through a tube, sort of like you were a deposit at the drive-up window of a bank. But this ... this was extremely pleasant, this sense of slowly rising and floating unseen above the heads of the shoppers. Away from the grand lobby, and through layer after layer of floors and ceilings until they found themselves in the toy department, nestled among a display of Santa's elves in a fake snow workshop.

Joe glanced around and—despite the crush of parents and children in the room—had no trouble finding his target. His picture must have been in one of his long-ago files, because Joe's eyes went straight to Colin. Tall, thin, well-dressed, elegant. British in that sort of Henry Cavill way that women always seemed to go for. Handsome in that sort of could-be-gay-but-God-help-the-rest-of-us-poor-slobs-if-he-isn't way.

And, just like Colin, the appeal of the Harrods toy department was evident at once. In a nutshell, they let the kids play. A dozen or so employees wandered around demonstrating various toys. Racecars zipped along the carpet, kites circled and dove overhead, electronic guitars strummed, dolls danced, and balls bounced. Colin and a Harrods employee knelt before a child in a bright pink coat, conspiring to amuse her by making a flower appear and disappear. Colin would pull the rose out from underneath the blue magician's cloth and then, with a flick of the wrist, make it disappear again.

The little girl was dazzled. She jumped up and down on her chubby legs, clapping.

126

"He's pretty good at it, isn't he?" Morgan asked mildly.

"It's not exactly hard to fool a one-year-old," said Joe. "I mean, look. It's a collapsible flower and he's folding it into his palm."

"I didn't mean he's a good magician," Morgan said. "I meant he's doing a good job as a father."

Joe, who was in no position to rate anyone else's parenting since he had never been one, looked at the scene more closely. Colin was on his knees before little Chance and, as he went through his simple tricks, his eyes never left her face. Every time she laughed, he beamed with satisfaction. Yeah, he was probably a really good dad, and yeah, that meant that Joe had been too quick to deem the guy a jerk. Besides, now that Joe was really considering the scene, something else was hitting him.

These people were young, in their twenties. All of them—Emma, Colin, Brodie, and Skye. Joe could hardly remember his own twenties, and that wasn't just because Transition played games with his memory. He could barely remember his twenties while he was in them. It was a time of uncertainty. A blur of seemingly endless choices made all the blurrier by sex, booze, and testosterone. His shoulders slumped. He knew what Morgan was getting at.

He had been too tough on Colin. Yeah, he'd bopped around a lot, but wasn't that expected, considering his age? Yeah, maybe he had ignored the big-hearted, sweet-faced local girl for the ball buster from the big city, but hadn't Joe made a similar series of selection errors? Or had he? His own past with women was as sketchy a memory as what had happened to his law partner.

He's twenty-six, Joe thought. Cut him some slack. Obviously, he doesn't have it all figured out, but who does? At least he's trying to be a good dad.

"Okay, maybe we do need to get him back and let him kiss Emma," Joe said, turning toward Morgan. But Morgan was gone. He must have collapsed upon himself and disappeared, just like the rose from the magician's kit. Joe was left talking to a mechanical elf, whose plastic hands were patiently wielding a foam rubber hammer to create more toys in Santa's workshop.

"So what happens now?" Joe asked the elf, who kept on rhythmically tapping.

Joe turned back to Colin, who had scooped up his daughter—along with a box that evidently contained the magician's kit—and had joined the long, serpentine line trying to take advantage of post-Christmas sales. Just as Colin was almost to the counter, a woman joined the pair.

Destiny Bane, Joe surmised. Attractive, if you like that high-strung, high-maintenance, big-city type. Thin almost to emaciation, the kind of thin that goes with being at the top of society's heap, thin enough that her clavicle was clearly visible beneath the skin, thin to the point of breaking but also rounded where it mattered and stylishly attired in a tight, dark dress and boots that went way up above her knees. Porcelain skin, raven-black hair pulled back to show a forehead elegant and high above a perfectly oval face. As she patted the little girl's head, Joe got a good look into large, dark eyes framed in thick lashes. Eyes that looked cold for all the smile on her scarlet lips.

There are all sorts of women in the world, each attractive in their own ways. Nobody knew that better than Joe. But how could Emma, who looked like a

128

schoolgirl, or even Skye, with her sweet, plump, always-flushed face, begin to compete with such a creature as this? He wouldn't have called Destiny "pretty." It was too mundane a description. Certainly she had a certain look— no doubt fostered and maintained, a look that spoke of conscious support. But there was something in her demeanor as well. "Attain me if you dare," it said. And few men could resist that. For a man like Colin, determined to take on challenges, Destiny must have been the challenge of a lifetime. Especially coming from the sweet wholesome likes of Skye and even Emma.

And she and Colin made a striking couple, Joe was further compelled to admit. Sort of a matched set. Both whippet-slim and dark, stylishly dressed. Colin had the little girl over his shoulder and his wife—evidently, she was still, despite their months of separation, his wife— languidly placed her hand on his other arm.

Well, this was trouble.

He and Alanna had been prepared to see it as a contest between Skye and Emma, two nice and (one might argue) equally deserving girls. But this Destiny evidently hadn't given up on the idea of retaining her hold on Colin. Surely she was on the way to convincing Colin to return to London and his family. Her hand on his arm managed to be both casual and possessive, a clear signal to the other women in Harrods that this particular attractive man was taken.

It's funny, Joe thought. *A man can see a woman's machinations so clearly when they're directed toward some other man.*

He watched the young family for a little longer and then decided it would be wise to find some private place, like a men's room stall, to materialize. He could hardly just pop up human among the elves. He was getting far better with the manifestations, Joe reflected, as he found an empty dressing room and was able to easily reclaim his body. During their first case, the manifests seemed like something that Morgan and his committee would thrust on Joe and Alanna without warning. A way to slide them around like pawns on a chess board.

But now, with a little practice, Joe felt he was becoming a more active participant in the manifests. He had been able to leave Alanna each night without making himself sick. Maybe it had made him feel sad and lonely, angry even, but it no longer made him feel sick. Besides, it was clearly what she wanted. The night Morgan had suggested they work strictly as business partners, Alanna had agreed so quickly that it had felt like a knife stuck between Joe's ribs. Oh, women could be so heartless. And after he had clearly shown her his feelings.

But, for now, he needed to stay focused. His mission had been to check out Colin's worthiness, and that mission had been accomplished. Now he had to get back to Alloway.

Joe walked out to the street. With so many people about, Joe figured he could easily manifest and dematerialize without causing a stir. He stepped into a recessed doorway, took a deep breath, and concentrated with all his might on the spot where he wanted to appear. The auditorium of the Alloway school. One ... two ... three.

Nothing.

Joe was not immediately alarmed. He'd gotten a bit better at it, true, but he was still hardly a master of manifestation. He took a deep breath and slowly exhaled. Took a moment to get himself completely present. Tried to remember what the teacher had said at the one meditation seminar he'd attended, probably spurred on by some woman he was trying to please—or get in her knickers, as they said over here.

There. Very calm and centered. One ... two ... three. Still in London.

Come on, Morgan, he thought. Show up and help me out here. I know I got a little cocky and tried to do it myself, and I'm sorry. You're still the man.

Eyes closed. Countdown.

Eyes open. A windy street in London.

Joe felt a small tickle of alarm. What if he was like Colin: stuck here in London? He had no money, no identification or credit cards. No phone to call Alanna, who had no phone to answer even if he somehow managed it. He could go to the airport, he supposed, and just hope a ticket was magically waiting for him. Or would the train station be better?

Morgan's trying to teach me something, he suddenly thought. *There's a lesson in here. Something about continuing to move forward even when the next step isn't precisely clear.*

Between the rain and the crowd, getting a taxi wouldn't be easy, but Joe gamely stepped toward the street, perched himself on the nearest curb and raised his arm. Within seconds one of the big black London cabs rumbled to a stop.

Now that's more like it, Joe thought. Morgan was undoubtedly at the wheel of the cab, chuckling that maddening chuckle of his and ready to scold Joe for thinking he was ready to use all the Wish Granter devices on his own. But when Joe scrambled into the back seat, he saw the driver wasn't Morgan. Just a typical balding, heavyset Londoner who glanced in his rearview mirror and said, "Where to?"

Where to, indeed?

"The train station," Joe said, with more confidence than he felt.

"Which one, then?" the driver asked with a bit of exasperation, as if Joe was another one of those dense American tourists.

Joe thought quickly. Indeed, where was he headed? The image of a small bear popped into his mind and he said, too quickly, "Paddington Station."

"Right you are," the driver pulled into the river of traffic and Joe settled into his seat. Had he been in London before, back in his human life? The city looked familiar but perhaps he had only seen it in movies or imagined it from books. The cab had an interactive screen in the back and Joe idly typed in a search for the train schedule from London to Edinburgh. Two transfers and thirteen hours, terminal to terminal. Great. Just great. But ... leaving not from Paddington but from King's Cross.

If he had to travel like a human—something that was beginning to seem like a great disadvantage—he would arrive at Edinburgh in the middle of the night and not make it back to Alloway until the morning. The morning of the thirtieth. Alanna would be beside herself with worry and there was no way to explain his absence to the townspeople of Alloway. Joe was surprised to find this was a large part of his agitation: the thought he might be letting down Reverend Dunn and the others.

It grows on you, he realized. This feeling of being needed, of being part of a team. And there was that nagging feeling again. That he had once been part of a team and that something had disrupted it. Had he left, been pushed out? Was it an amicable departure?

Of course, there was another whole issue: the issue of money. He was going to the train station on the flimsy hope that a ticket would be waiting for him there, but if he was betting on Morgan to have arranged something, wouldn't it make more sense to hope that the ticket came in the form of an airplane ticket? Flight times to Edinburgh were less than an hour. Joe took one final look at the computer screen showing the route by train and quickly made up his mind.

"Excuse me," he said to the cab driver. "I've decided to go to the airport, not the train station."

The cab driver shot him an incredulous look over his shoulder. "Which airport?"

"Which is closest?"

"Seriously, man, do you know where you're going, because I'm not ..."

And then it happened. The cab driver, thinking he had a lunatic for a passenger, twisted in his seat to observe Joe more closely. And, distracted as he was, failed to see the yellow light. The cab rolled through the intersection and right into the path of an oncoming truck.

Horns. Lights. The sickening sound of rubber skidding across pavement. Joe may have had time to cry out, but he wasn't sure. He saw the gray wall of the truck moving closer, sliding, utterly out of control, and then he was gone, lifted out of that black London taxicab and back into his little Porsche in Boston.

He had been so proud of that car. Used, but still ...

It had been dark green. Black bucket seats. He'd had the sound system upgraded the moment he'd bought it. What was playing that day? Rock music. Loud. Van Halen maybe, or The Boss. He had been singing. Yeah, Springsteen. "All That Heaven Will Allow," now wasn't that a joke? He'd been happy and at ease, and then ...

That truck. The truck in Boston. The one that had seemed to come out of nowhere with such speed and such force but no sound. The truck that collided with him that morning in Boston had not made a sound. There had been no squealing tires, no horn blast of warning.

Then Joe was floating. Out of the cab, out of his body. He felt that familiar slightly nauseous feeling that seemed to come with involuntary transport, but there was no doubt anymore why he had been brought to London. Seeing Colin was useful, sure, but that was just the ruse. Morgan had really brought him here and left him on his own because it was time for Joe to have another memory—and this one was a whopper.

He looked down at the intersection below him and noted with relief that the truck had stopped short of actually hitting the taxicab. The drivers of both vehicles were out in the street, furious and yelling but unharmed. It would be some time before his driver even noticed that the foolish American who didn't know where he wanted to go was already gone.

But a mystery had been solved. On the day he had been driving his Porsche through Boston, talking on his cell to Vera at his office, he had not had an accident. Yes, he'd been hit, but there was nothing accidental about it. The driver of that truck did not swerve, did not skid, did not apply his brakes or even his horn. It had all come back to Joe with the undeniable force of fact.

Someone had wanted to kill him. That truck was the "how," but what was the "why"?

134

The wind was shifting, picking up moisture from a powerful vortex that hovered as if awaiting instruction.

People speak as if storms just happen, as if they hit suddenly, without warning. But that isn't the case. A storm is a patient thing, building with tenacious resolve. Each has its own destination and intent. Each has its own personality with particular characteristics. Once it gets on a set path, it's beyond the power of humans to alter or stop it. Joe was in the middle of just such an event. Perhaps not cosmic in its power, but certainly relentless.

FIFTEEN

Destiny turned away from the window and said, "Stay. It's not worth the risk. Even if your flight does leave on time tomorrow, who can predict the condition of all those rutted little country roads? Half of them are impassible even in summer ..."

Colin came up behind her and also looked out the window. The fog outside (or was that snow already?) was so thick that he couldn't see the street just seven stories below. Destiny's penthouse apartment—his too, until only a few months ago—was the perfect retreat from the December chill. Enormous fireplaces, high, paneled ceilings, a series of Oriental rugs across rich, chocolate-brown floors. The stocked refrigerator, with dozens of small white boxes holding tasty, elegant little treats they'd picked up from the market level of Harrods and every kind of beer a man could imagine, could sustain them for days. His daughter was napping in her room, still clutching the magician's cloth in her hands, and just a bit farther down the hall was the master suite. The recessed lighting and overstuffed chairs, the tub with its bubbling jets and steaming water, the high soft bed fluffed with eiderdown comforters where he and Destiny had once slept together as man and wife. The bed in which they had conceived their child.

It was all so perfect, as if designed for a stage set. And enticing. No doubt about it, this was the quintessential holiday scene. The ideal city apartment, just like the one he'd dreamed of so many years ago—when living in

London and working as an actor was all he wished for, all he wanted. *What a fool I'd been*, he now thought. But he'd grown up in a simple cottage where there was never quite enough room, never quite enough water pressure, never quite enough heat or light nor quite enough excitement or encouragement for what he really loved. For Colin had his own wishes—and no one to help him fulfill them. That is, until he had met Destiny one day when he was down in London. "A chance meeting" she had called it with a wide-eyed giggle, tossing her hair about and touching his arm. He'd always had a way with girls. But he'd never met one who had a way with him. He would have followed her to the Moon and back.

He was the perfect mark for Ms. Destiny Bane. Handsome in a way the Londoners she was used to lacked. It was that fresh outdoors look about him. The ruddy cheeks and dark mop of hair. The piercing blue eyes and easy gait. The way his tall frame seemed to fit in no matter where he went. This was the perfect consort for the woman who had lofty goals, who wanted power and all that went with it. She didn't want a man who would thwart her ambitions, nor did she choose to be an armpiece for some titan. No, she would choose a man who could fit in nicely at any club or table, in any drawing room, and especially on the cover of any magazine as she carefully crafted her inevitable rise. She had big plans, and the right man was essential to fulfill them.

Destiny was still gazing at him, the look on her ivory-pale face expectant. When she'd asked him to stay, did she mean for another day, until the storm passed? Or had she meant forever?

"You must be hungry?" she said in her clipped, proper English. She'd gone to all the right schools, of course, made sure her pedigree was unquestionable.

"Are you?" he answered.

It was a clumsy attempt to stall, and a foolish question. Destiny was never hungry. The ritual of food was yet another way to control a situation.

"Not yet," she said, walking toward the kitchen with a smile. "But I'll fix you a plate if you're feeling peckish. What would you like? Perhaps the short ribs? Some of the risotto? What about some of that pickled mushroom salad or maybe the asparagus?"

Her voice trailed off as she turned into the kitchen, and Colin settled back down on the couch. Destiny had been working very hard to make this Christmas nice and to give him all the things he'd complained he never had enough of when they'd lived together as man and wife. Suddenly now she was pouring time and attention all over him—and Chance too, so much that the child seemed confused by her mother's constant presence and kept asking for her nanny. Suddenly there was food and life in the apartment, time together as a family, and Colin wasn't sure, but he suspected that Destiny had even engineered the supposedly accidental meeting at Harrods with his former boss.

In the beginning, he had been as guileless as a lamb before Easter and hadn't suspected her of any motives other than to make him happy. And she had willingly allowed him to think that about her. She even thought how dull of him to expect her to stay home and play housewife while he was out looking for work. Or what passed for work. Auditions. How idiotic, she'd thought but kept her counsel about it. Endless auditions. She even made sure to take him to a few parties where he'd met a number of producers and even some movie people. He learned that he would have to take acting classes. And should have a voice coach. And the dancing was really not a priority these days. But his voice was a plus and he could carry a song. Perhaps, it was suggested, he should think about a singing career. Then one of them had offered *her* a screen test. As if she'd be interested in that sort of thing. She quickly determined that Colin must have a good, solid, steady job where he couldn't get into trouble or have these dreams fed by a lot of unreliable types who always seemed surrounded by curvy young girls with big ambitions.

Finally, he'd met an agent who took an interest in him and got him a bit part here and there, some radio commercials and even a brief stint on a TV series playing a politician's assistant. But the series never took off and he was back to auditions.

Destiny grew irritated with his stop-and-start shenanigans, so she wheedled him into a bank job, insisting that they needed stability at home. She told him he could still go to some auditions on his time off. And maybe he would land a real part one day. Eventually this had split them apart. Colin wanted to give it a good try, but Destiny said it would ruin their marriage—especially if he did get an acting job. Imagine, she'd said: He would be away every night. They would have no family time. And then she threw in the final assault. Their baby would never see her father. That was no way to raise a child.

When they ran into his old boss at Harrods, Colin tried to be cordial and avoid the subject of how he'd left to pursue parts. But the man asked right out how it was going, and that was an open door for Destiny to bolt through. She told him Colin was not finding work and explained how difficult it was to get a good start in theater these days.

The boss listened politely and then offered to take Colin back anytime he wanted a place at the bank. Everyone had liked him so much, the boss had said. And the customers still asked about him, especially the ladies— the elderly ones with big accounts always asked if he was returning soon.

Destiny had beamed. "See," she'd said, as they'd told the man to have a happy new year and hurried along their way. "You haven't been forgotten. You can still step right back on the career track."

Career track? That was a laugh. Colin's job at the bank had been boring and repetitive. Not a position likely to lead anywhere more interesting, and certainly not to the sort of earning capacity of Destiny's at the law firm. The only good thing you could say about his job was that it had ended each day promptly at five, allowing him to spend evenings with Chance, which was especially vital on those numerous nights when Destiny worked late. So much for her argument about family time. She left most of the child care to one of those high-priced British nannies who came with reams of credentials and letters of recommendation. But, he had told himself, while a position in customer service at a bank was hardly an exciting career, it was a good enough way to earn money and spend his days between auditions. Because Colin had never totally given up the dream of acting on stage. The London stage. Real theater. The bank had been a stopgap on his way to bigger things. Most actors held other jobs when they started out, so why not him?

He thought that Destiny understood this. It was only by accident that one day he'd overheard her on the phone laugh and say, "It's a bit of a toy job, but it keeps him off that bloody stage."

And suddenly he saw the full picture. The job she'd claimed to have heard of through a work associate had really been prearranged for him. It was a way to keep him out of the theaters—a career aspiration that his wife deemed silly, even embarrassing, a way to make sure he put on a suit every day and left the house at a reasonable hour, that he appeared to be doing the traditional husbandly duties. He'd noticed that, when they went to an office party or were out with friends—her friends, never his, since Destiny proclaimed that the theater crowd suffered from "a pathetic degree of self-delusion"—that Destiny was often vague about the exact nature of his work. All her friends knew was that he worked at a bank. It was a socially acceptable post for the husband of an ambitious solicitor, and that was all the public needed to know.

They didn't need to know he was not in some posh office and that he was dying of boredom and kept one eye on the clock until he could leave every day. That he couldn't wait to audition for some small touring production of an experimental play or go home to be with little Chance.

Colin looked around the room. Oh yes, it was perfect, no doubt. The Christmas tree, the fire, the soft sounds of holiday jazz wafting from the expensive sound system. As well planned as a stage set, which was precisely what it was. Destiny had created this tempting taste of the perfect city life to get him back. Everything from the beer selection, to the fact she'd sent the nanny on holiday, to the way she'd arranged to run into his former boss. It was all contrived to remind him of what he was giving up, designed to convince him to stay.

Because Destiny Bane did not intend to be dumped by a Scottish farmer or to suffer the social stigma of losing custody of her child. For her to star in the life story she'd planned, she needed the tall, well-dressed husband and the adorable bouncing child. He and Chance were as much a part of her props as the catered short ribs and professionally decorated tree. The comfort all around him was temporary and illusory. Like Brigadoon, it would all soon disappear.

"I would love to stay," he called into the kitchen, knowing it wasn't true even as the words left hovered in the air. "But you know Aunt Aileen is mad to see Chance over New Year's. And of course they're expecting me for the play."

"Auntie can see the baby just as well next week," Destiny promptly called back. "And I don't know why you've let them all convince you they can't do that silly play without you there. Didn't you say Brodie knew the part as well as you do?"

That silly play. He'd told her a dozen times how much it meant to him. It didn't matter that he wasn't paid for it, or that nobody important—no casting director or theatrical agent—would ever see him in the role. He didn't care that the scenery was painted by his old third-grade teacher or that the only musical accompaniment was a creaky old piano and a thunder of bagpipes. Or even that the story, upon even the most casual reading, didn't make much sense. Brigadoon represented home to Colin. Security, family, childhood. His father had played Tommy before he had died, and perhaps someday his son ...

But no, another of the things Destiny was stalling on was more children. For a female solicitor with her eye on a plum political prize, one child was mandatory—a sign that she was, despite her ambition and intellect, still maternal and nurturing. But two or three children was excessive, unnecessary. Colin looked around him. His choice was clear. His life in London with Destiny might have looked good on the surface, but the reality of it had been sterile and lonely. He wouldn't stay, but neither could he leave baby Chance here on her own to be cared for by a nanny who would either spoil her through overindulgence or, more likely, discipline the spirit out of her.

Destiny was back at the door—a plate of food in one hand, a beer stein in the other. Was it his imagination, or had she unbuttoned the top of her blouse? "Besides," she said airily. "It might all be out of our hands. I heard on the news that, if the storm moves any more inland, they will have to close Gatwick." Oh, she was so offhanded about it all. As if stranding them together was an act of God she could not control. "So we might as well enjoy ourselves. I've missed you so." She said this with a wistful little smile and leaned down rather farther than necessary to hand him the plate of food. "We did get on so well together for a while. Remember, Colin?"

What could he say? Colin thanked her and accepted the plate. He knew the food was probably delicious, prepared by one of the best chefs in Chelsea, but it felt thick and tasteless in his mouth. She had a way of moving him from obstinate reluctance to tacit agreement, and there seemed nothing he could do to change that. Ever since they'd separated, he'd felt that pull back. She'd let

143

him go, but there were invisible strings that tugged at him. Little Chance was one. But the others were always her knack for seduction coupled with the solicitor's ability to see many sides of an issue and focus on the one that will win. So she continually lured, badgered, argued, seduced. And he gave in more than he intended. They'd made love many times since the separation. Not that he wanted it. But he simply couldn't resist her. This troubled Colin more than anything else between them. He derided himself for his weakness and swore it would never happen again. Now here she was, bending over, offering him food and, it was obvious, more.

She was undoubtedly right about the storm. The wind had grown so blustery the windows rattled as sleet pounded steadily against them. If the airport closed, there was no way to Edinburgh, to Ayr, and on to Alloway. He and Chance would be stuck right here for days.

He frowned, took a deep gulp of the beer. Destiny was a very determined woman, a polished solicitor, an ambitious pol-in-the making, and she possessed acting skills he had to admire, knowing that this was all a performance for his benefit. But even she wasn't capable of creating a storm.

She sat beside him on the small sofa and placed a hand lightly on his knee and, with her other hand, took his hand and locked fingers with him and turned so she could look up directly into his eyes.

"Tell me you haven't missed any of it," she said, "and I'll believe you."

"Dez," he began. "Why are you doing this? Especially tonight. You know I'm torn. But you also know I can't live the life you want of me. I'll never fit into your sort of world. And the other world of acting draws me more and more. I know you want us to be together, but you must realize the facts of it. Don't you?"

She took his hand and raised it to her lips and kissed each finger in turn. He had never been able to resist her, and she was sure she could work him again if she offered up enough incentives. And try she would. Besides, a snowy night, howling wind, warm fire, and her own determination to get what she wanted was more temptation than she could resist. And why should she anyway? He was her husband: strong, virile, more willful than when they first married it seemed, and these traits made love-making all the more pleasurable. Let him resist. She would wear him down, make him angry, then let him do whatever he needed to dissipate that anger.

Sixteen

Alanna handed the pile of clothes to Dunn, saying, "Here are the costumes. I'm sure it's always possible to do more, but Skye and I made a pretty good start."

"Thank you, my dear," Dunn said. "Now sit and watch this patch, tell us what you think. We can always use a pair of fresh eyes."

Alanna turned back toward the seats and was somewhat surprised to see Joe waiting there.

"Where have you been?" she whispered and slipped in beside him. She almost reached out to take his hand but drew back at the last minute.

"London." He could feel the warmth as it radiated from her body, the scent of her lilac perfume in the air reached him and he wanted to turn and kiss her, so glad was he to be back with someone familiar, someone who understood him, who shared this experience of whatever it was they were sharing. He wanted to tell her about the truck and hear her thoughts about it. And then his thoughts slipped seamlessly into her own experience and he wondered what had happened, back there when she was alive. What had brought her to be in Transition with him?

"Were you there with Morgan?"

"Yeah, and ... you were right. Colin's an okay guy." He settled down. They were here and everything would be all right soon.

"Morgan took you all the way to London to show you that?"

146

Fortunately, at just that moment Dunn signaled Emma and Brodie to start the scene, and Alanna's attention was pulled back to the stage. Joe sat in silence, pretending to be transfixed by lines of dialogue he had heard many times before. He wasn't sure why he didn't tell Alanna about the close call in the London taxicab, or his memory that his own death had been far from accidental. Maybe later there would be a good time.

His law partner had been gunned down in front of their office in broad daylight. There had never been any doubt that his case was a revenge killing. So there must have been police, right? An investigation and maybe an arrest? Joe closed his eyes and tried to concentrate, even though his brief time in Transition had taught him that concentration was not necessarily the best way to tap into memory.

Russ had been shot and then, merely months later, Joe's own car was run off the road. If there had been detectives and an investigation, they must have immediately seen the connection. Joe tried to recall the last cases the two of them had worked on, to zero in on the client whose conviction—or possibly release—had prompted such a violent reaction. How long ago had this happened? When he and Alanna had been on their first case in Las Vegas it had been spring but, now, a blink of an eye later, here they were with Emma in Scotland in December. Had eight months really passed since his death or was time measured differently in Transition?

It was entirely possible his case wasn't closed. That some detective in Boston was still trying to figure out who had killed him, and why. Or maybe it started somewhere else beyond Boston. Some bigger city. Someplace where his poor partner, Russ, might have gotten drawn into something more dangerous than he'd expected. The violence had spilled over into their practice and rubbed up against Joe without his knowing it.

Joe was aware that his entire body was tense, that he had clenched his fists and tightened his jaw. This new knowledge was a tricky thing to have in his possession. If he went back now, what would be his goal? Justice? Revenge? Or simply a need to know how his story worked out? The simple need to know isn't really that simple, Joe realized. It was what had pulled Emma to Scotland, and it was what would someday pull him back to Boston—or beyond.

The action on the stage had paused and Alanna turned back to him. "So what did you see in London?"

"I went to Harrods, wound up in the toy department. Saw Colin with little Chance. Morgan was there, hanging around next to the queen in a portrait. I think he just wanted to make sure I understood that we can't ruin one person's life to make everything right for another. Oh, and I also saw the wife."

"Ex-wife."

"Not quite yet. We can't blind ourselves to the fact Colin is still married. And it's my feeling that the lady isn't utterly prepared to give him up." Joe sighed deeply. "I told you this story needed a villain. Someone who is evil through and through, someone we can both rally against and destroy. I was trying to make it Colin, but that just doesn't fit. Maybe it's Destiny, the wife."

"You're talking like a lawyer," Alanna said, gazing up at the stage. "Automatically assigning blame to the other side. But there's no reason to assume Destiny is evil."

"She calls herself a lawyer," Joe said, still bristly. "But I can tell just by looking, that chick has never been to the

148

mat. Never got the call to come bail a client out at three in the morning, never done the old wheel-and-deal, never closed in front of a jury that's half-asleep. She's all estate planning and mergers, the clean bloodless stuff—and still she calls herself a lawyer."

"Actually, she probably calls herself a 'solicitor,'" Alanna said. "It's the British term, isn't it? Why do you care what sort of cases she tries, or what kind of woman she is? Even Skye doesn't blame her. Besides, our focus isn't in London. It's right here."

Emma was standing center stage now, surrounded by the gaggle of village women, evidently aged eighteen to sixty, who were meant to represent her sisters. Not all the casting was terribly persuasive, and Alanna thought back to Skye's remark that Dunn dreamed of making the play a grand, year-long affair, bringing in busloads of tourists. Could Alloway manage such a task? Was the town even big enough to make it work? Parts of the play were wonderful, and other parts—this scene, for instance ...

Emma began to sing. Her voice was not particularly strong, but it was true and clear. Something about how she wouldn't settle for just any man. That she wouldn't marry until she found the man of her dreams, even if it meant waiting for her sweetheart until the end of time. The lyrics made Alanna's chest hurt.

"Besides, what's wrong with talking like a lawyer?" Joe said, still indignant. "At least in court, it's all marked out clean and plain. You know who you're arguing for and who you're against. Who's the accused and who's the injured party. But this mess ... everyone seems kind, and sort of wounded. Everyone's deserving. We've got four people and one wish. How the hell are we going to work all this out?"

Just then the doors of the school opened and, to Joe and Alanna's surprise, Brodie came in carrying Skye. He brought her to the front row of seats and carefully lowered her, then spread a blanket over her legs. Dunn walked to the center of the stage and clapped his hands to get everyone's attention.

"Alright, Skye is once more with us," he said, "and that means everyone is here. I called this town meeting because the time has come for us to make some decisions. To consider what happens if Colin is unable to make his way back from London tomorrow in time for the performance."

For a moment, the room sat in complete silence. Alanna thought that, on one level, everyone was prepared for this possibility and, on another, they found the idea of *Brigadoon* without Colin almost incomprehensible. The first person who dared to speak would set the tone for the whole meeting.

"Is it definite he won't be back?" a man asked.

Dunn sighed. "Barring a miracle. The news reports that both Gatwick and Heathrow are iced in. Perhaps you should call him, Aileen, and urge him to make the prudent choice. I don't see him attempting to fly under these conditions, especially if his child is with him."

"He won't take the chance with Chance along," Aileen said firmly. "Not even if they open the airport to flights tomorrow."

"Well, then, Brodie shall play the part; that's obvious," said Skye, her voice calm and self assured. Cast or no cast, Colin or no Colin, she seemed relieved just to be out of the house and part of the play in whatever form that took.

"I'm not as good as Colin," Brodie said. "And there's still a chance ..."

Dunn interrupted him before he could finish. "Always a chance," he said, "but I think we must be practical. And besides, Brodie, your voice is just as fine as Colin's. The dancing is different, I will admit, but where Colin bests you in agility, you take the prize in terms of strength. You feel comfortable dancing with him, do you not, Emma?"

Emma looked up, startled, as every pair of eyes in the village suddenly fixed on her. "Yes," she said quickly. "Quite comfortable."

"Colin's the actor," Brodie said stubbornly.

"Aye, and how much acting does the part require?" Dunn asked with a shrug. "Far be it from me to critique our dear play, but the lines are not exactly Shakespearean. How hard is it for a young lad like yourself to pretend to be in love with a pretty girl?"

Emma flushed. Brodie looked away.

"Besides," Joe pointed out. "You don't have anybody else."

A burst of laughter shook the room. Joe could always be counted on to state the obvious.

"As our American friend so rightly points out," said Dunn. "Brodie is our only right and proper choice. There is the problem of costume, of course. Brodie has at least three stone on Colin ..."

Three stone, thought Alanna. Mentally she wrestled to convert that to pounds.

"We have several extra costumes," she ventured. "Perhaps with some alterations ..." She spoke a bit timidly, since she didn't want it to seem like she and Joe were a pair of outsiders who showed up full of ideas and tried to take over. Alloway had been doing a New Year's performance of *Brigadoon* for decades without any help from them.

"Aye, but those are the Scotsman costumes," said Dunn. "If Brodie is to persuade the crowd in the role of Tommy, he must look like an American on holiday."

Joe frowned. "Which means?"

"He must wear the things the British think of as being uniquely American," said Emma, suddenly understanding the stash of Levis and T-shirts she'd found in Colin's closet. "Joe, you're not far from Brodie's size. Do you have anything he might borrow?"

"I never go anywhere without my Boston Red Sox sweatshirt," Joe said doubtfully. "And I think I have a T-shirt from Tufts."

The minute Joe said the words he knew they were true. That's where he'd gone to law school. Another memory located.

"Brodie can do an American accent," Aileen broke in. "Knows them from the telly, don't you, love?"

"I suppose," Brodie said skeptically. During the last four days of rehearsal with Emma, he'd been speaking in his normal voice. He closed his eyes, trying out a line or two in the more aggressive rat-a-tat rhythms of American speech. Or maybe Joe could help him get it right. Joe seemed the most American of all the Americans he'd ever met.

"I don't wish to be negative," Joe said slowly, "but the Reverend raises another point. He said that if Brodie is to convince the crowd ... but will there still be a crowd? The same storm that's locking Colin in London might keep our audience away."

An uneasy silence fell on the group.

152

Interesting, Alanna thought. *He said, "our audience" instead of "your audience." He's invested in this little performance too, just as much as I am.*

"It's a small percentage of our crowd that comes from London," a man said. "Most are Scots and need not fly ..."

"All the rooms in the town are reserved," a woman said.

"Reserved, aye," Aileen responded. "But that's no guarantee our guests can make it over the highland hills and into Alloway. Joe makes a sound point. Even if we put on our show without Colin, what's the purpose if no one can come?"

An even deeper silence descended.

"We could postpone," said a man.

Dunn flinched. The idea obviously did not sit well with him.

"Brigadoon has always been performed on New Year's Eve," Skye protested. "Every year of my life since I can remember and probably long before that. It's a magical night, is it not? A night when anything is possible, when we all agree to believe in things we canna yet see, a night when the whole world agrees to hope ..."

"Skye's right," Emma said resolutely. The English teacher in her was awakening and she pushed to her feet and moved to the front of the church to stand beside Dunn. "Yes, there may be a smaller crowd due to the storm, and yes, you may have not have the usual leads ..."

"Listen to her," Joe whispered to Alanna. "She's completely willing to do the play with Brodie instead of Colin. What happened to her wish?"

"It changed," Alanna whispered back. "It grew up."

153

"Swell," Joe said. "But where does that leave us? If Colin doesn't even make it here, do we still get credit for this case?"

"With everything on the line, that's what you're worried about?" Alanna hissed back. "I swear, Joe, you make me so angry sometimes. Can't you put the practical on hold for a little while with all this romance in the air?"

"New Year's," Emma was continuing, "is the perfect time to present this story. The only time to present it, because, just as Skye says, it's a night when there's magic in the air. A night when we all stand suspended between the past and the future, with one foot in two different worlds."

"That's all well and good for her to say," Joe whispered, leaning in so close to Alanna that she felt his warm breath on her neck. She trembled, struck by feelings she couldn't totally deny. "Come New Year's Day, she's on a plane back to the States, and, if the play was a financial flop, it isn't her problem. She can afford to be all romantic about it. These people can't."

"If you postpone a few days ..." Joe said, this time speaking much louder and directing his comments toward the whole group. "Even a couple of days would give the storm a chance to lift and your audience a chance to travel."

Dunn, however, was already shaking his head. "On January the second," he said, "the whole world will turn back to business, to travel, to work, to school. We really have no choice. There is a very small window of time in which a sentimental little play like ours can touch the heart. During the holidays, people are soft and open. They have their families around them and enough leisure time that they might travel to our humble Alloway to be

154

convinced that true love conquers all. But then January comes upon us and that window snaps shut. Reality is once again the dominant impulse of our lives. And who cares to look for Brigadoon then?"

Dunn looked directly at Joe, his small blue eyes sharp and piercing against his weathered face.

"No," Dunn repeated. "Skye and Emma are right. There are so few hours in the year when the curtains part and we are willing to believe. Very few chances for the impossible to become possible. And one of those times is midnight, New Year's Eve. That is when our play must end, just as it has ended for so many years. And if there are but a dozen people in our audience, we can do no more than pray those dozen people are moved. That is all our Lord sent out, is it not? A dozen simple men into the world to spread His message?" It was almost a sermon from the reverend.

The small crowd erupted in applause. Dunn hugged Emma, who slumped against him like a daughter to her father.

"So, fine, the play goes down tomorrow night as planned," Joe muttered to Alanna. "We've got all the magic and emotion you can shake a stick at. But no Colin, no crowd, no computers for the kids, and no wish granted unless you and I figure out something fast. Where is Morgan when we need him, anyway?"

"Last seen in London according to you," she muttered back. "But the town doesn't just need to do the play to make money. It's also their tradition, their identity. How they define themselves. When Morgan said the play was how they continue to exist, I think he meant they need it emotionally as much as they need it financially."

155

"Joe," Dunn called out from the stage. "Since everyone is here, perhaps we should go through the wedding scene and end with the ringing of the midnight bell. Do you mind?"

"My big special effect," Joe whispered to Alanna before he nodded and sprang to his feet. The bell on the stage, the one Skye had been hanging when she fell, was just a prop. It didn't even have a clapper. At the climax of the play, just before Brigadoon sinks once more into the mist, it was Joe's task to climb the bell tower of the church next door and give out twelve slow and distinctive peels. Evidently in the past this had been one of Brodie's tasks, but since Brodie was subbing for Colin, Joe had to sub for him. Dunn had assured Joe that the distant sound of ringing bells was a very effective way to close the play. The bells would ring and the lights on the stage would gradually fade, leaving just the shadowy figures of Fiona and Tommy, on the verge of an eternal embrace.

Joe dashed up the aisle, out of the school, across the frozen yard and into the church. The steps to the tower were a steep, narrow climb and, by the time he arrived, he was out of breath. He thought about the days when he'd played football and wondered briefly when in life he'd gotten so out of shape. Or maybe it was being in Transition that had turned him from fab to flab. One more thing added to the list of Transition mysteries that deserved a confrontation with Morgan, he thought.

Joe peered down and saw the boy who was to be his signal standing in the door of the schoolhouse. Everything was in place. He sat down on the spindly wooden chair to wait for the signal. From way up there, he could see the whole town: the stone bridge over the river Doon, the snow-covered yews and pines, the roofs of houses, the chimneys of the Robert Burns cottage, and the old Kirk ruin.

And then ... strange. In the distance he could see a car coming. Moving so smoothly toward the village that there could be no one other than Morgan at the wheel. So that's where he's been, Joe thought. Still playing cabbie while this whole case was collapsing like a pillar of sand.

The car eased over the bridge and down the road, and finally the driver pulled as close to the school steps as possible. It was a dark sedan, one of those chauffeured Bentleys that are designed to be unobtrusive. The sort of car a politician would use to tool around town with his mistress. Not flashy like a Rolls, but almost as expensive. The sort of vehicle which conveyed the most refined and understated type of elegance.

But that couldn't be Morgan. Joe frowned. Hard to believe a car like this was even available in this humble part of the world.

The driver leapt out and opened the door behind him. Not Morgan, Joe realized. Not even close.

A woman emerged from the car, tightly wrapped in a sleek black coat trimmed in dark fur, a hat pulled low to obscure her face. She looked neither right nor left and certainly not straight up toward the bell tower, but Joe could have sworn he'd seen her somewhere before. Something about her form was familiar. She moved fast and then Joe realized the boy at the door was frantically waving his arms and it hit Joe with a jolt that he'd almost missed his signal. He leapt to his feet, nearly conking his head on an exposed beam as he rose and began to pull the rope attached to the bell. It hadn't occurred to him how frigging loud it would sound from up here. It was a miracle Brodie hadn't gone deaf over the years, because the noise hit Joe's head like the clap of a cymbal. He winced but kept ringing. On the fourth peal he saw a pair of foam earmuffs hanging from one of the beams, but it was too late to stop now.

By the time he finally got to twelve he was gasping—both with the effort of pulling the rope and the trauma of the noise—and once again realized how out of shape he'd gotten. Now he turned back toward the schoolhouse to be sure he was doing all right and he saw the woman in black at the top of the stairs where the boy who had been Joe's signal held the door open for her. The woman paused on the stoop, carefully removed her hat, and shook loose her long black hair.

Then Joe knew where he'd seen her. But no, it wasn't possible. The London airports were all iced in. Dunn had confirmed it. And Joe knew for a fact that it took thirteen hours to travel from London to Edinburgh by train. There was no way Colin could get to Alloway, so how could she? Now here was another topic to cover with Morgan the next time Joe saw him. The topics were piling up, stacked one atop the other, and Joe's patience for the whole situation was worn to a nub.

SEVENTEEN

It didn't take long before Joe's opportunity to confront Morgan arrived.

He, Alanna, and Morgan were seated in Alloway's hideaway pub, slamming back ale with a steady determination. Alanna noted that, for the first time since she'd met him, even Morgan seemed mildly rattled. He kept glancing toward the window, with a wary expression she'd never before seen on his face.

"I don't get it," Joe said. "How did she get here and what does she want?"

"What she wants," he said, "is to help Dunn and the others. She's come bearing money."

"What sort of money?" Joe said. "Where did she get it?"

"Oh, from some charity I'd imagine," Morgan said. "She was in charge of the holiday fund drive for her law firm, or perhaps she sits on the board of some arts council. Something high profile and publicly commendable—the sort of organization where ambitious people congregate. Most of the funds go to projects in London, of course, but perhaps there are a few pounds left over to help a struggling theater group in some far-flung little corner of the kingdom. All sold as a tribute to the town where the famed poet, Robert Burns, once lived and wrote. And drank, as I recall."

"Wait a minute," Alanna said. "She's come to help underwrite the Alloway production of *Brigadoon*? Why? She hates the town and she hates the grip it has on Colin."

But Joe was ruefully shaking his head. "It's brilliant," he said. "The kind of win-win solution lawyers are always seeking. At least on the surface. She swoops in on the eve of the big production in a year where it seems like the Alloway Players are all but washed up for the year. Who cares if the play draws a crowd if there's a big arts council grant from London to cover the costs? And if she can guarantee a steady stream of money—peanuts by the standards of a London art gallery or theater, but big money by Alloway standards—she becomes the local hero. Colin no longer has to feel guilty about deserting his hometown in their hour of need. He stays in London with the wife who pretends to be supporting his dream at the very moment she's keeping him right where she wants him. So Destiny gets everything she wants and is declared the Saint of Alloway in the process. Yeah, bloody brilliant, as the Brits would say. I'd like to have a smart shark like that in my law firm if I ever get back to the land of the living." He looked straight at Morgan, then continued. "And while we're on that subject, I have a few tasty bones to pick over with you."

Morgan finished his beer and raised his mug for another, all the while looking steadily at Joe as if to say, "Go ahead. Knock yourself out."

"Of course, the big one is when do we get a shot at going back?" Joe held up his hand and shook his head, knowing that was one question that would inevitably go unanswered. "But second to that, what is really going on with this Destiny character? I mean it's gotta be obvious she's no ordinary hausfrau. And this solicitor pose seems equally fishy to me."

"I have a question," Alanna broke in. "Will Dunn go for this deal she's offering? I mean, I'm with Joe: It all

160

seems a bit too convenient. And her showing up in the middle of a blizzard ... well, if she's not on your team, then what gives?"

The barmaid brought his new mug of beer and he spent some time studying it.

"I wasn't going to mention this but, since you're both so eager to know the ins and outs of things."

"Yes," Joe said. "We're both eager, especially since it impacts how well we do on this mission. I mean, if we have someone working against us ..."

"Destiny Bane is not exactly working against you specifically," Morgan explained. "More like she's working against me and the Transition Committee and all the positive things we're tasked to do. She works against anything that's not in her self-interest or that positively impacts anyone else related to her self-interest."

"Why?" Alanna asked.

"That's a difficult question. She's what you might call a 'thwarter.' She thwarts others in order to further her aims." Morgan set his mug down on that table and looked around. "It's rather a more intricate equation than we have time to delve into at this point, as we have these other matters to resolve."

Joe was not satisfied, and he began to say something, but Morgan held up a hand to stop him.

"It's not only an intricate equation and a matter of urgency but also a question of cost benefit. The cost for you to know the full extent of Destiny's reach at this time has been deemed not to benefit your mission here. Emma is your main concern. Destiny will have to take a back seat."

"Which leads us right back to her offer to Reverend Dunn," Alanna said. "Will he accept it?"

"Why not?" Joe asked. "It's the answer to all his dreams, isn't it?"

"His dream wasn't just money. It was a standing theater and a series of productions that went on all year and the chance ..."

"... to make money." Joe shot her an incredulous glance. "Dunn would be a fool not to welcome her with open arms."

"Sometimes what looks like a gift is really a yoke," Morgan mused. "Anyway, we'll know soon enough," Morgan said. "She's meeting with him in his office at the church even as we speak."

"But that doesn't answer the bigger question," Joe said. "Not why is she here, but *how* is she here? I know for a fact from my time in London that she couldn't have come by plane or train."

"So what does that leave?" Morgan asked.

"Car," Joe said promptly. "Which I saw, but if she'd driven from London that would have taken, I don't know, at least as long as a train, and she was there this morning when you and I were in ..."

"Or manifest," Alanna said quietly. "She could have come by manifest."

"Manifest is what we use," Morgan explained.

"We as in Joe and I?"

"And Morgan," Joe offered. "Anyone else?"

"Maybe we're not the only Wish Granters," Alanna said. "I mean, there must be others."

"I'm not authorized to tell you everything," Morgan said. "But I can tell you this: For every act of positive energy there is always an equal act of negative energy. I don't mean in some cosmic way, although I suppose that's also true. Above my level, so I don't concern myself with

162

such larger issues of the universe. I must leave that to others. But Transition can be a very crowded space full of all sorts of opposing forces. Whether Destiny Bane arrived by car or camel caravan is of no importance. What matters to us is, will she achieve what she's come here to do, which is to thwart Colin and therefore Emma?

"So there are other ways to appear and disappear? Not only by manifest?" Joe was stunned. "She's some sort of spirit moving among the living and doing who knows what to them?"

"Her name," Alanna was saying warily. "Means more than it seemed. I suppose she's somebody's destiny, but hopefully not Emma's. We've missed a lot here in tiny Alloway."

Joe was still doubtful. "She can't be a spirit. Colin must have known her for years. She lived in Alloway, slept in his bed, became pregnant with his child, gave birth. Did all the things a human woman does."

"You two know as well as any that, when a spirit manifests on Earth in human form, its body does all the expected things," Morgan said. "Right now, for example, I am nearing the end of my second pint of ale and wondering where the water closet might be. And you two have had the same experience, have you not? You've eaten, slept, bathed, wept, sneezed?"

"You left out one really important human experience we haven't had," Joe pointed out.

"Oh, God," said Alanna, ignoring another of Joe's reference to sex. "Are you telling us she's some kind of witch?"

"Wait a minute," said Joe. "Are you telling us we can still have sex?"

"Try to focus," Alanna snapped. "He's saying that this woman—or whatever she really is—has lain in wait for years just for the chance to destroy not only Colin but also Alloway and everyone in it. The goodness that we saw when we got here ... she saw it too, didn't she? And it enraged her. She set a plan of revenge into motion. She knows that, if she destroys the heart of the play, she destroys the heart of the village and that there's just one less spot of kindness and decency left in the world."

"So if we have sex," Joe said to Morgan. "Will it be exactly like human sex, or will it be more, you know, spiritual and kind of intermingled?" His eyes were bright at this thought of some new kind of sexual experience after all this waiting.

"For God's sake, Joe," Alanna said, so loudly that half the bar patrons turned to look. "We've got to warn Dunn. Tell him who, or what, he's really dealing with."

"Don't worry about Dunn," Morgan said. "He's more clever than you might guess and most definitely on the right side of the battle. Are you sure this is how you want to spend our limited time together?"

"No," Alanna said firmly. "You've got to tell us more. Because Joe is right, Destiny lived with Colin for a sequence of human years, which would imply she is limited by the walls of human time. Like having a baby, for example. That takes nine months—a very human form of measurement."

Morgan sighed. "Ordinarily it would be too early for me to be telling you this, but I didn't figure she would be here this soon ..." He nodded at them soberly, took another sip of ale. "It's a tribute to you both, really—a sign that she thinks you're good enough at this to make it interesting. Worthy adversaries even though this is just your third case." He sighed again, sipped again.

"Time ... means nothing in this arena," Morgan continued. "You've undoubtedly noticed that much at least. What seems a year in a human's life might be no more than a second in Transition. The time it took her to gestate a child may have been nine months for Colin and no more than the intake of a breath for her."

"I see where you're headed," Joe said, struggling to pull his mind away from the little party that had been going on inside his head for the past two minutes. So sex with Alanna was still a possibility, but it didn't seem likely unless he got back on board with this present case. She kept shooting him angry little glances and biting her lip. He needed to pull himself back to the game going on right now.

"If Colin is measuring time in a human sense," Joe continued, "it's safe to assume he's still in London and unaware that she's even left. He might think she's in the bathroom or taking a nap."

"It's even worse than that," Morgan said. "She can be many places at once. Can dance with a dozen men in the same ballroom, and each of them will see a different woman's face. She can ride in a thousand backpacks into the same battle. North or South, East or West, Nazi, Boer, Confederate, Rebel, or Militia, it makes not a whit of difference to her. She whispers her promises to them all. And she is seductive in the way of the most successful courtesans of history. She makes each man feel special."

Joe slumped. "A woman who knows how to make a man feel special is the most dangerous force in the world. She can get him to do whatever she wants."

"And Colin was a sitting duck," Alanna said. "He performed on the stage from the time he was a young boy, so he must have always been driven to seek attention. But being a big fish in a town like Alloway would have meant nothing in London. He was probably reeling with shock at being a nobody, one of just hundreds of hopeful actors. If a woman like Destiny singled him out ..."

"That crazy name, Destiny Bane," Joe said. "It's like she was trying to give herself away. I assume she goes by many names, depending on the situation?"

Morgan nodded. "And in the future I wouldn't count on her making it so easy for you."

"In the future?" Joe said. "So she might show up in the middle of other cases? What's in it for her?"

"Sport," Morgan said. "A mental challenge, a game. Eternal life can get very boring, you know. And there's no better distraction than dabbling in human affairs. Humans provide the most varied field to entertain the Destinies of the—what shall I call it—not 'the afterlife' exactly, but perhaps 'the hyper life.' Humans provide drama, comedy, mystery, and romance, all available all the time. And humans all want something they do not have. They are all subject to wishes. Nothing gets Destiny's blood flowing like a human wish. She delights in the challenge, in thwarting the one who wishes. And she has chosen to pit herself against the Wish Granters, to intervene in ways that keep the wishes from coming true." He drained his mug and lifted it to show the barmaid he was ready for another.

"You drink a lot," Alanna said abruptly.

Morgan nodded. "I do like my beer. And the occasional margarita."

166

"How does she keep wishes from coming true?" Joe asked, draining his own beer. He had said the story needed a villain, but now that one had appeared, he felt betrayed and angry. Good spirits and bad, both capable of interfering with the hopes and fears of humans. The nuns had been right about more than he'd given them credit for. Nuns? Where did that come from? Another vague memory reference. He must have gone to Catholic school at some point.

"Oh, you've undoubtedly experienced her presence in your lives on many occasions," Morgan said amicably. "She rarely comes in at the beginning of a wish. She waits, bides her time. Her goal is to punish humans for daring to have wished in the first place. She wants to drive them back into self doubt, cynicism, sarcasm, procrastination, despair." Morgan grinned. "All the frailties to which humans are especially vulnerable. And she knows the best way to punish humans for being foolish enough to hope is to show up just when they're on the verge of having that hope realized. She comes into the story late, in other words. She's the plateau dieters hit when they're ten pounds from their goal weight. The old girlfriend who comes into town just when the guy is finally ready to propose to his new love, the flu that strikes the day of the big job interview, the flat tire on the way to the airport, the fumble on the five-yard line."

"The truck that comes at you on your way to work," Joe said under his breath.

Alanna sat in silence. Sure, everyone had those moments. But they always thought it was just bad luck, not the machinations of an unseen evil force.

"There are few things more disheartening than the setback which arises just when it seems the dream is about

167

to be reached," Morgan said. "And she understands this, which is why she sits and waits. Of course, she does have other strategies, such as the one she's undoubtedly using with our friend Dunn at this very minute. She has been known to offer a compromise deal, something close to the original wish, at least on the surface, but which somehow fails to deliver the true heart of the thing. In this case, she is offering Dunn a way to save Alloway, but it's a salvation from outside, come from London with strings attached, and Dunn's true dream is for Alloway to save itself. Whether or not he falls prey to her offer remains to be seen. But I'm betting on him to make the right choice."

"We can't warn him?" Alanna asked. "We can't tell him that he may be entering a bargain with—what should we even call her? Is she the Devil?"

Morgan's face took on a quizzical expression. "I'm not familiar with that term."

"Oh, come off it," Joe said. "We're obviously involved in some sort of struggle between good and evil, and this chick is obviously on the side of evil. Is she always female, by the way?"

"She is capable of taking many forms," Morgan said mildly, as the barmaid placed his fresh ale in front of him. "But yes, she is usually female. At least as far as you two are concerned. You have been assigned only women's wishes so far, after all."

"That's the Devil all right, "Joe muttered. "When I first saw Destiny in Harrods, I felt it. Something about her was awful, but something else was appealing. Even while I'm shaking my head and thinking that both Emma and Skye are prettier, nicer girls, so much more deserving of his love, even while I was thinking all that, I could see why Colin would want her."

168

Alanna cocked her head. "Does she work alone?"

"Not exactly," Morgan said. "Her victims are also her assistants. The minute she manages to plant doubt in their minds, they rush to help her complete her grim mission. The dieter figures, since she broke her vow over the salad dressing, she may as well have the cake. The man with the flu refuses to reschedule his big meeting, shows up sick for the presentation and pukes on the potential client. We suspect our lover of straying, so we turn into such vindictive, irrational fools that they do stray. We're so exasperated about missing our flight that we drag our bad mood behind us and ruin the whole trip. One fumble leads to another. You humans hardly need a devil plotting to destroy your dreams. All it takes is for our friend Destiny to show up at a key point and either frustrate you or tempt you with a shortcut and, bam, you do the rest for her."

"You're saying we self-sabotage," Joe said. "That, in the end, we destroy our own dreams."

Morgan nodded. "It's the true curse of the human: that quality of self-sabotage given the slightest push. Those of us in Transition—call it what you please, the spirit world, Heaven, angels, or demons—like to dabble in human affairs, but we don't really have the kind of influence that humans imagine. The Wish Granters can set something into motion, but where it goes and how long the change is sustained falls squarely into human hands. And our friend Destiny can merely divert dreams in the most momentary sense. The human decides whether or not her little games mark the end of the wish or only a temporary setback."

"Does she have any vulnerabilities?" It was the lawyer in Joe, looking for a weak spot, a way to unravel the witness on the stand.

"Only one."

"What is it?" asked Joe, for one day he might really need to know.

"Her ambition."

"Let's just hope," Alanna said grimly. "That Dunn is as strong in his faith as he is in his directing and that he stands firm."

EIGHTEEN

Dunn, a man not given to confusion, was, for the moment, flummoxed. "Your kindness is overwhelming," he said. "I scarcely know what to say."

"That's the easy part," Destiny said. She sat across from his desk in the pastor's study, her pricey designer scarf tossed back from her shoulders in a careless gesture and her long, slim legs, encased in shiny black leather boots, neatly crossed. "You just say yes."

"Ah, lass, but that's the one thing I canna say. Alloway is run by a town council and a decision such as this must be put to a vote."

Destiny's eyes narrowed slightly, and she leaned forward. This one was tough, this church man. She frowned and said, "I don't see what the problem is. It's an offer of money, pure and simple."

"And there's the trouble," Dunn said mildly. "In my experience an offer of money is rarely pure and never simple. I shall call a meeting of the council, shall I not? And have you your answer before nightfall?"

Destiny glanced out the small window. "Nightfall is here."

"Just a trick of the eye, lass," Dunn said. "Common to these regions at this time of year when the days are short, when the shadows fall so fast, and it can seem that mere afternoon is almost midnight. But I assure you, things in Alloway are never quite as dark as they seem."

"So what do you think?" Brodie asked Emma. "It's found money, and unexpected funds are always welcome. But Dunn must have some reservations about it or he wouldna asked the council what they thought. We're kind of a figurehead organization, at best."

"How often do you meet?"

Brodie shook his head, and his dark unruly hair bounced. "I canna remember the last time."

"So there's your answer," said Emma. "If Dunn told her he couldn't take the money without speaking to the council, it was obviously a stall. Something about it doesn't feel right to him. Look, I probably shouldn't even be the one you're talking to. It's not my town, and it's easy to make grand gestures and speeches when you don't have anything on the line ..."

"I want your opinion," Brodie said, spreading his hands wide. "You've seen more of the world; you have the formal education I lack. You might think of aspects that would not occur to me. Why is she here and what does she really want?"

"You have the Colin disease," Emma said, with a short laugh. "It must run in the MacGregor family."

"And what, pray to Mary, is the 'Colin disease'?"

"You think that education is a matter of the places you've visited or whether or not you went to college. How much money you earn, silly things like that."

Brodie looked at her with his chin down like a man wearing reading glasses. "All right, then—don't give me your opinion as a woman of the wider world; just give me your opinion as Emma, simple and true."

"I don't think Destiny is doing this out of any love for the arts," Emma said. "Or because of some lingering devotion to Alloway."

"Aye, that much is obvious."

"It's her way of hanging on to Colin, keeping him in London. And improving her reputation in Alloway in the bargain."

"And again I will agree. Even Dunn, with his limited knowledge of women, saw that much. But the question is: Even if the money comes with tainted intent, should we still take it?"

"Why does the town do this play?" Emma asked.

"You know the answer as well as I. For money."

"Just for money? How much could a single performance take in each year?"

Brodie shrugged, knowing he was caught. "I canna say. Five hundred pounds last year, if memory serves."

"Not enough to keep a town going. That's what you tell yourself: that what drives you to perform *Brigadoon* year after year is the need for money. Yet you only make enough for a computer or two for the library, little things like that. How did you spend the five hundred pounds last year?"

"Patched up the street," Brodie said guiltily. "And I know it must sound very foolish to a woman who teaches at a grand school, who knows all about ..."

"First of all, I might teach at a grand school, but the salary they pay me is nothing," Emma cut in. "And secondly, I don't think it is foolish. People often start doing something for one reason and continue doing it for another." Emma knew this much from her own experience. She had come to Alloway seeking Colin, but that wish now seemed as insubstantial as a snowflake. But

173

Brodie was waiting for her to continue. His large, brown eyes—so dark they were almost black—fixed on her face.

"For example," she said, continuing after a short intake of breath, "the citizens of Alloway say they do their annual performance of *Brigadoon* as a fundraiser. You've been saying that to each other for so long that no one questions it anymore. It is just your comfortable explanation for why the show must go on. But I think you really do it because the tradition is what holds the town together. You look forward to it every year. Everyone chips in. It's an excuse to spend Christmas as a family."

"We could still do the play even if we had a grant from a charity."

Emma shook her head. "Are you sure? With the money would come actors from London, a theater to maintain, an audience that would expect you to mount a performance like one they might see in the East End. They would expect all the bells and whistles, and not ..."

"Not a bunch of moth-eaten plaid costumes and out-of-tune bagpipes and a farmer in the role of Tommy. That's what you're saying, isn't it? That if we take the money, it won't be our *Brigadoon* anymore."

Emma started to protest then figured there wasn't any point. That was exactly what she was saying. Destiny may have come up with the plan merely as a way of keeping Colin in London, but a charity-funded *Brigadoon* would soon cease to be a simple, hometown production. She merely nodded.

"You're right, of course," Brodie said quietly. "Dunn knows it, too, else he wouldn't have come up with the stall. He just didna want to be the fat one, as you Americans say."

174

"The fat one? Oh, you mean he didn't want to be the heavy. Okay, so perhaps you'll have to be the one to break the news to Destiny. How did she get here anyway? I thought the whole point was that the London airports were closed."

"Said she was in Scotland anyway. On business."

"That makes no sense," Emma said, shaking her head. "What sort of lawyer business could she have in Scotland on December twenty-ninth? You all are a very trusting little family."

"Perhaps we need someone to keep us wary," Brodie said. He had dropped his head but not before Emma caught the twinkle in his eye. "Some cynical soul who looks out for our business better than we can ourselves. A woman from America, perhaps."

"Perhaps," she said quietly.

They stood for a moment in an awkward silence. The stage was cloaked in darkness, and the auditorium was completely empty. Empty, that is, except for Emma and Brodie.

"Are you nervous?" she asked him.

He smiled shyly. "Should I be?"

"I mean, are you nervous about the play?"

"I know what you meant."

"Well, I guess what I'm really asking is ..."

"What are you asking, lass?"

His voice was low and husky. It was one of the most attractive things about him, Emma thought. That, and his long dark eyelashes. Or maybe his full bottom lip. "You know the songs and the dancing," Emma said. "Better than Colin, isn't that what everyone's been whispering in the wings all week? But you don't know the lines, do you? You've been reading from the book all week."

Brodie chuckled. "You think I don't know Tommy's lines, front and back? By Jesus, I've been listening to my cousin say them all my life."

"But the book ..."

"Was so I could cue you on your part, love. I may know Tommy's lines, but I don't know Fiona's."

"Love." He had called her "love." Of course, it was a common endearment in Scotland. Dunn had called her "love" this very afternoon, and Skye used the term for everyone from Morgan to her cat.

Nonetheless, the word emboldened her. Emma reached out, put her hand on the rough cotton shirt stretched across Brodie's chest. They were standing downstage left, beneath the tree, beside the rock. The part of the stage where Tommy first kisses Fiona.

"So you do know the words?"

"Every one."

"And do you know the staging? Do you know, for example, what happens here, beside this rock?"

He leaned toward her, moving so slowly that, for a moment, she thought perhaps she was imagining that he was moving at all. It was an agonizingly protracted journey, as if his lips were crossing an ocean to meet hers, as if they were taking years to arrive.

And then he kissed her. Not privately or secretly, not in the shadows or under the pretense of being a character in a play. Brodie kissed Emma long and deep and openly, on the shadowy stage.

This was different, she thought. Or sort of thought, since she had the strange sensation of simultaneously being in her body and being lifted above herself, looking down and observing. Colin had been smiling as he kissed her, long ago. It had been a teasing kiss, a kiss that had a

176

question implied behind the sweetness. *You do see it, don't you?* the kiss had asked. *You see how special I am, how dashing and different from the local boys? You do realize that you're a lucky girl to have been singled out, do you not?*

And then, the other kisses through the years ... nice enough, sometimes more than nice. But they were too often just a prelude to other things. The acknowledged way that sex starts, the accepted opening move a man is expected to make. He may find it pleasant but certainly no place to linger. A couple of minutes and then on to what guys consider the good stuff. She had always felt their impatience, even in the ones who tried to hide it.

But kissing Brodie was some new, fresh, unexpected experience. The kiss was whole, complete in itself. It had no hidden expectation and no hidden message. It said hello and goodbye all at once.

She pulled away, gasped for air, then leaned in and kissed him again. He murmured something against her lips and she answered, a moan of a response.

And then, from far away, another sound. A single person, clapping.

Brodie pulled back but kept his arms around her. They squinted in the darkness toward the sound.

A woman—dressed in black with her equally black hair pulled away from her perfect, pale face—strode toward them down the aisle, clapping her hands.

"Lovely," she said. "And very touching. I'm sure the audience will be completely convinced."

All the air seemed to have gone out of Brodie, but he tried to sound casual. "Ah, Destiny," he said. "How goes it with my favorite cousin-in-law?"

Oh no, Emma thought. This frightening creature was Colin's wife? In an instant, Emma sized her up. Chic.

Rich. Sure of herself. Demanding. And here she was mooning over Brodie. But maybe this creature thought they were only rehearsing one last time. No, she must have seen the whole thing, Emma's hand reaching for Brodie, the kiss with no embrace. The way they held it longer than needed. The yearning there and the satisfaction. This woman in black was, without a doubt, the worst person on Earth to have caught them kissing like that.

"My favorite scene in the play," Destiny said, her lips turning up in a smile that had about it a mix of revenge and contempt and something else: some hint of triumph. "You can't imagine how much I enjoyed it, watching Colin kiss that chubby little hausfrau year after year. Where is Skye, anyway? Has she given up the part finally?"

"She's been hurt, if you must know," Brodie said. Now that he was over the surprise of seeing Destiny, he seemed stronger. He dropped his arms from around Emma but, pointedly, did not introduce her. She understood. She walked to the wings of the stage and busied herself with unlacing her high black boots. "And you didn't watch Colin and Skye in the play year after year. As I recall, you only lived in Alloway for a single season."

Destiny shrugged one shoulder as if to push off an annoying bug. "Time is a very relative thing. It seems as if I've sat in these wretchedly uncomfortable chairs in this dark damp hall for half my life, listening to the bagpipes wail like a herd of wounded moose and farmers leap about in their bathrobes, calling it a highland fling."

"If the play's so dreadful, why have you come offering to save it?" Brodie asked.

Again the superior smile. "Heaven knows why, but this town means something to Colin," Destiny said.

"Which is why I hope you'll put aside any past animosity between the two of us and urge Dunn to take my offer. When he said he had to call a meeting of the town council, I knew that really meant he just wanted to run the matter past you. He holds your opinion in such high regard."

"Heaven knows why," Brodie said, matching her sarcasm.

"I haven't come to insult you, Brodie, or to insult Alloway or even your little play."

Destiny glanced around the room and the stage, her eyes coming to rest on Emma. "It's obvious you're struggling as it is, making do with whatever substitutes you can find. This one's new to me." She took in Emma with one intense stare and then went on. "Just promise me you'll consider the offer." She approached the stage and, to Emma's surprise and horror, climbed the steps.

"So this is what it feels like to be an actress," Destiny said, standing center stage and turning slowly in a circle to take in the clutter of props in the wings, the painted scenery behind her, then the seats in front. "Can't say I see the appeal." She reached out abruptly and laid one of her pale, thin, hands on Brodie's forehead.

"Are you all right, cousin?" she asked, her voice dripping with fake concern. "You seem a little flushed. Whatever would they do if you happened to get sick, too? Now that would be a real shame for little Alloway."

Joe was almost out of town when the Bentley sped past him. The wheels churned in the snow, spewing slush in his path, and he jumped back with a curse. It looked like Destiny wanted to get out of Alloway in a hurry, and he supposed that was a good sign. Dunn had evidently not caved, and Joe could just imagine her fury. But Joe was suspicious, given everything Morgan had told them, that she wouldn't give up so fast. If Dunn rejected her first offer, the lawyer in her would be compelled to come back with another. If the town rejected all her offers, the devil in her would seek revenge in some other form. Revenge. It was terrifying to contemplate all the forms that might take. But Joe had no idea how far her powers could reach.

There was Alanna standing on the bridge. He knew this somehow even before he'd begun his walk. No matter where he was or what else was happening around him, some part of Joe's consciousness was always monitoring where Alanna was and what she was doing. They had been in Alloway, what, four days? Or was it coming up on five or six? It was so hard to keep track of time here. But Alanna had come to this bridge every day, had stood just as she was standing now, her gloved hands clasped over the railing, looking down into water running just below the thin veil of ice that seemed never ready to completely freeze over.

Joe's heart suddenly pounded as he watched the Bentley skidding across the bridge, the driver not slowing to accommodate the narrowness or the fact that Alanna was there. She jerked with surprise at how close the car passed by her, but the threat was gone as fast as the car came, and Joe was left with a half-scream stuck in his throat. Cars scared him now, ever since the stint in London and the memory of how he had died. He must tell Alanna all this sometime soon. It would help her understand why he was so determined to return to his old life in Boston. Why it was so important that he find some kind of justice.

He continued to plod toward her. They hadn't seen much of each other since they'd come to Scotland, at least not compared to their first case where they had clung together like angst-ridden teens. Yeah, Morgan had warned them to keep their minds on their task, and that was part of it, and it also made sense that—as they gained more experience as Wish Granters—they would begin to operate independently of him so they could complete their tasks using only their own intuition, come up with their own solutions.

Joe thought of the plot of *Brigadoon* and of all the kind people he and Alanna had met since they had come to Alloway. With the notable exception of Destiny—who he still thought of as a devil, or maybe a witch—they were all nice, sweet, earthy people. Each one deserving happiness and love. Yet even here, in this idyllic place, something could keep them from the love they longed to have.

Their romantic troubles seemed to stem from the most basic sort of difference. Distance. Proximity. Living apart from each other. Too far apart to make daily contact or establish the kinds of routines that hold people together. Joe knew there was more at stake here than mere geography. The seemingly simple question of "Your place or mine?" in reality meant decisions that determined the daily realities of their lives. Yet people could live under the same roof and still be miles apart. If love truly conquered all, then miles should not make a difference. Joe knew this was rarely the case—that love was not a static thing that never changed. It had to be nurtured, fed, lived. Loving someone was like a child two people shared.

Without constant attention, love could fade and dry up like a leaf in winter.

It was beginning to dawn on him that he and Alanna were in the same boat. He was running toward something, and she was running away from something else—and, despite the fact that neither of them could articulate exactly what they wanted or feared, there was no doubt that they were moving in different directions. They both knew it, which was probably why they had both agreed so readily to Morgan's suggestion that they keep their distance from each other. Painful as it was, it was better than facing heartbreak that he now thought awaited them down the road.

Alanna looked up to see Joe standing beside her. The softness of the snow was like a blanket, muffling sound. She hadn't heard him approaching and had no idea how long he'd stood there observing her.

"Looks like Destiny has left town."

Joe nodded. "Looks that way."

Alanna turned back and leaned over the rail of the bridge and watched the sluggish movement of the stream leading back toward Alloway. Alloway, which also seemed immobile and unchanging but which, beneath the surface, held all sorts of activity. The hopes and dreams and pain of each individual human heart.

Joe came to stand beside her, shoulder to shoulder, and leaned on the rail. She was aware of the presence of his very human body pressed into hers. Solid and masculine and comfortable to feel beside her. Alanna sighed and moved just a little closer, allowed her side to slump into his. It had been so long since they had really touched.

182

"Would this be enough?" Joe asked. "This simple, sweet life where every day is just like the one before it? Or would a woman eventually get tired of paradise?"

Alanna pulled her scarf a bit tighter and stared back at Alloway. "I think Emma could be happy here."

Joe shook his head. "I wasn't asking about Emma."

NINETEEN

Skye McFae didn't have to leave her house the next morning to hear the biggest story in town. All she had to do was hobble to her door and open it to let her cats out. Immediately, she was struck with the accustomed chill in the air and the unaccustomed bustle in the village. Cars inched their way along the street, and clumps of people navigated the just-swept sidewalks, pulling suitcases behind them. The audience was beginning to trickle in, from Edinburgh and beyond. Maybe not as big a crowd as usual. The loss of the Londoners would surely have its impact on the till, but at least the seats would not be empty.

But that wasn't the news. The news came in the form of Duncan Dufree, a local boy in his last year at the school and bound for a trade academy in Ayr on graduation. He was helping a woman, probably one of his mum's overnight boarders, with a suitcase when Skye pushed open her door. A storm may have been brewing in London, but you couldn't prove it here. The sun on the snow was so blindingly bright that Skye had to shield her eyes. In the crisp air, even the cold felt good on her skin.

"Morning, Skye," Duncan called out. He was a cheeky lad who'd on occasion made no secret of the fact he wouldn't mind a tumble with an older woman before he left for the bright lights of Ayr. "You've heard, I suppose?"

"Heard what?"

"Scuse me, ma'am," he said to the lady and sprinted across Skye's tiny yard, his boots sliding on the ice.

"Brodie MacGregor," he whispered, loud enough that half the town could have heard him. "Sick as a dog, laid up with the fever."

Skye nodded numbly and shut the door with a thud. She leaned against it, her cast stuck straight out in front of her, the wind knocked out of her at this news.

Colin stuck in London. She breaks a leg. Now Brodie struck down with fever, coming mysteriously and suddenly on the very day of the play. What was happening to them? It was almost as if the production had been cursed.

Skye hopped awkwardly to the phone and picked it up. It wasn't as if she didn't know how to reach Colin. Through it all, the many ups and downs of their long friendship, they had always talked. In fact, they had always understood each other. In the past week especially, there had been so many times she had thought of calling. When Emma showed up. When she fell. Brodie taking the role. The unbidden and incomprehensible appearance of Destiny. All things he should know—and worthy of a phone call—but something had always stopped her from dialing.

And still she hesitated, even now. Skye placed the old phone back in its cradle. She wouldn't call, wouldn't try to persuade or whine, wouldn't push him toward one decision or another. If Colin ever turned his eye to her, ever asked her to be his wife and Chance's mother, she wanted to know that the choice had been his and his alone. She had waited a long time, true enough, but she still had her pride. She was Skye McFae and she deserved to be a man's first choice, not the thing he settled for when the rest of the world had kicked him in the teeth.

But now with Brodie sick, Colin missing, and the clock on the church steeple ticking away the time steadily toward the moment when the curtain would rise, what on Earth would happen to the play if they didn't have a Tommy? Who on Earth could step into the role on such short notice? Dunn? Duncan? One of the farmers who scarcely had the range to carry the demanding role of Townsperson Number Six?

Skye opened her desk drawer and pulled out a candle and, with it, a card she'd been given only a few days ago. Not one of the usual candles she had setting about because she liked their scent or the warm glow of candlelight in the evening. This candle was slender and white, a taper such as a church would use, and Skye carefully wedged it into its tiny stand. She lit a match and closed her eyes.

She wouldn't call Colin, but there was someone she could beseech for help. Divine help, that's what was required.

"So," Dunn summarized for the hastily assembled group of players. "We find ourselves in a bit of a pickle."

Pickle, my ass, thought Joe. How many more setbacks could this small production survive?

"Emma's still hale, is she not?" asked a woman from the crowd. "'T'would be a horror if she got sick as well, and I understand she and Brodie have been working very closely."

A low titter of laughter ran through the group and, tired and worried as he was, even Dunn managed a smile. There were no secrets in a town the size of Alloway.

186

"Aye," said Aileen. "She assured me over breakfast she feels strong as an ox. But I bade her to go back to bed anyway, and rest. No use in taking any chances with her health, or to make her sick with worry."

"Praise God," said another woman. "Whatever Brodie has then, it isn't catching."

Emma is only well because Destiny doesn't know who she is, Alanna suddenly realized, but she couldn't very well say that aloud. God, how stupid could they have been? Morgan kept trying to warn them, and still somehow she and Joe had failed to connect it to Destiny. The woman—if "woman" was indeed the proper word—who was not only determined to thwart Emma's wish but the wishes of everyone in Alloway.

She's the one who knocked Skye from the ladder, Alanna thought, with a sick thud in the pit of her stomach. She's the one who ensnared Colin and cursed Brodie with a fever. The only reason Emma has escaped her wrath is because—for some reason—Destiny had not yet figured out who Emma was. Or perhaps—this was a long shot, Alanna thought, but possible—Emma was under the protection of the Wish Granters. The shaky protection of Alanna and Joe and the rock-solid protection of Morgan. Or so Alanna hoped. But in the pub, even Morgan had seemed a bit cowed by the power that Destiny seemed to wield. So Emma truly was, as of this moment, Alloway's only hope to pull off this year's production.

"So our Fiona is fine," Dunn announced, cutting into Alanna's meandering thoughts. "But what do we do for a Tommy? I think the answer is clear enough to us all ..."

"Hear, hear," said a man. Townsperson number whatever.

"He has the Tufts T-shirt, after all," said a woman.

Tufts T-shirt? The thought hit Alanna and Joe simultaneously. They both went stiff and looked up in horror.

"We've asked so much already considering you're but a guest in our town and not coming here expecting to be so put upon in so many ways," said Dunn, as he walked slowly toward Joe. "But you've answered every call we've raised, and we can only hope the answer will be a 'yes' once again. You will be our Tommy, will you not?"

"I'm no actor," Joe said with an expulsion of air. "I swear to you, putting me on stage would be the end of ..."

"You have the American T-shirt," Townsperson Number Two said calmly.

"A costume doesn't make someone an actor."

"You know the lines," Dunn pointed out. Joe started to protest again, but then he realized what the man said was true. In all the rehearsals, all those times he had stood in the wings managing the props, he had somehow known the lines. Not just Tommy's, but all of them, the entire script of *Brigadoon*. Joe had no idea how he knew these things. He could only assume that the playbook had been included somewhere in Emma's file—the file he and Alanna had somehow absorbed when it was handed to them by The Committee, before they were whisked back to grant Emma's wish. So much of what had happened was still a mystery. One day, Joe assumed, all the gaps would be filled and all his questions answered. Until then, he just had to play along.

"So I know the lines," Joe snorted. "I can't dance or sing."

"We'll lead you through the highland fling," said one of the men. "And the ballet is mostly lifting Emma, spinning her around. You've watched it all week, have you not?"

"Watching and doing are two different things," Joe howled. Dear God, it appeared these people were actually serious. "Besides, faking dancing is one thing. You don't want to hear me sing."

"Try it," Dunn gently urged. "'What a rare mood I'm in ...'"

Joe sighed. They weren't about to take his word for it. The arrival of Emma had convinced them that all Americans were heaven-sent and blessed with significant talent. He stood, took a deep breath, and bellowed.

"What a rare mood I'm in ..."

"All right, that won't work," said Dunn and the other villagers were likewise shaking their heads. "Ideas, people? Thirty, perhaps forty, members of our trusting audience are already here as we speak. We dare not disappoint them."

"Two years ago, we recorded the show," Aileen said slowly. "The tape is in my kitchen drawer I believe. And Colin's voice is on the tape."

"Aye," said Dunn. "You're right."

"I can't lip-sync along with Colin's voice," Joe protested. "That sort of ruse can go wrong so easily, and when you mess up, it looks so stupid ... just ask any American pop star. Trust me, lip-syncing is nothing more than a fast way to look like a fool."

"We'll get the tape," Dunn said forcefully. "We'll bring Emma here and spend the afternoon practicing the dancing and the singing and ... "

189

"It won't work," Joe said. "The audience will see through me in a second."

"Probably so," said Aileen. "But Joe, love, you're all we have."

"What about ringing the bell? I'm supposed to do that."

"Aye," said Dunn. "'Tis a simple thing to get one of the lads to take that on. This is far more dire, don't you see?"

By ten in the morning Colin had packed both his bag and Chance's on the minuscule chance that the storm would lift and they could get to the airport and on a plane. Now there was nothing left to do but pace and wait and monitor the situation via the telly news.

"You're driving yourself mad for no reason," Destiny said, coming in from the kitchen with a scone in her hand. "It's getting worse, not better."

"Only in London," Colin said grimly, staring at the muted television screen. "If we can get out of the city, we'll be fine. The trains are running."

"You've waited too late for that," Destiny said.

Was it just his imagination that her voice sounded smug? She wandered down the hall with the untouched scone. But irritating as she could be, Destiny was right. If he was going to make it into Scotland by train, he should have left yesterday. But he had been so dismayed at the thought of a thirteen-hour train trip with a one-year-old in tow that he had decided to wait and hope that the weather would clear enough for them to fly.

190

So much for that. He glanced back at the screen, noted the time. The play would be starting in precisely ten hours.

Chance came toddling toward him with the bright blue cloth from the magic kit in her hands. She had found dozens of gifts under the tree, a ludicrous amount for a child her age, and she had frankly shown more interest in the boxes than the toys. But she was enchanted with the pieces of that silly magic kit. For the past three days, Colin had been using the blue cloth to cover things—a shoe, a cereal bowl, a book—and each time he had yelled "Abracadabra" and pulled back the cloth, Chance had squealed and clapped her hands.

"Aba," she would say. "Aba."

Now she handed him the cloth and he obligingly dropped it over the nearest item, which happened to be a piece of pottery on the table. Something tribal and rough and undoubtedly expensive, one of Destiny's finds from a fashionable art gallery. "Abraca ..." he started and then he was interrupted by Destiny, who was now dressed and carrying her briefcase.

"Tell me you're not going into work today," he said.

"Just for a couple of hours," she said, opening the closet to pull out her coat. "Darling, did you bring your nice suit with you? You know, the one I got you for your birthday last year?"

She knew he hadn't. "Why do I need my nice suit?" he said, being careful to keep his voice neutral. Chance may have been little more than a baby, but she was sensitive to tones and mannerisms. She was right now standing between her parents, looking wide-eyed from one to another, as if measuring the tension level between them.

"Well, the firm's New Year's party is tonight, and I would dearly love to have you by my side, especially after last night." She smiled up at him, an alluring smile that promised more of the same. "Of course, getting a sitter at this late date could be difficult but not impossible, for enough pounds I suppose."

"We don't need a sitter," Colin said, smiling through gritted teeth. "Because, if you recall, Chance and I are on our way home."

"Home?"

"Home."

Destiny's face never changed expression, but she inclined her head toward the television screen, where footage of the storm was running nonstop. "And what is your plan for getting there?"

"We could rent a car ..."

"And arrive sometime tomorrow morning, if you're lucky. Really, Colin, we'll have to discuss all this later, but I do wish you'd consider coming with me tonight. I have one very brief meeting and then I'll be back. Perhaps the three of us can go to lunch." Destiny kissed the air in the general direction of her daughter, picked up her briefcase, and walked out the door.

"Aba," Chance said.

"Okay, darling," he said, turning back to the table and the blue cloth. He shouldn't let Destiny get to him like that. True, it wasn't looking like he would get back in time for the play; he knew that Brodie could sub for him in the role. Brodie would be fine, Colin knew that. Skye would be there to help him through the rough spots. He wasn't entirely sure what was compelling him to go back to Alloway, with a baby, in the middle of a snowstorm.

"Aba," Chance reminded him, tugging at his pants leg.

He muttered some nonsense words and waved his hands while Chance watched with solemn eyes. She was so little that it didn't bother her that he was merely covering things up and revealing them again. She seemed dazzled every time he pulled back the cloth, as if having the full attention of her father was magic enough.

"Abracadabra," Colin said, pulling the cloth away with a flourish.

The bowl had disappeared.

Chance clapped her little hands. Colin frowned. Where had that old bowl gone? Had it rolled off the table while he and Destiny had been sparring? He looked around, even dropping to one knee to peek under the couch but still no bowl.

The doorbell rang. Scooping Chance up and still looking for the bowl as he walked, Colin moved to answer it. He assumed it was Destiny, returned for some item she'd forgotten for the office. He pulled open the paneled door with one hand only to find, on the other side, a rather oldish (but you wouldn't say "old" exactly) black man wearing a cap. He was smiling affably and nodded his head twice.

"You called a cab?" the man said.

"Wrong flat," Colin said, starting to close the door. But the man slipped in a hand to stop him.

"Cab to Scotland?" he insisted. "Reasonable rates."

"No one takes a cab to Scotland," Colin said, a little startled. Who had sent this guy? Was this Destiny's idea of a joke? If so, he wasn't about to play her little game.

"I assure you, my rates are so good you can't afford not to go, and I will make very good time," the man said. "Ask Chance, if you don't believe me."

"How do you know my daughter's name?" Colin demanded. The guy seemed harmless enough, but this was all very strange. "Why would you offer to drive me to Scotland?"

"Did you drop this?" The man extended a creased brown palm toward Colin. In the middle of it was a piece of tribal pottery. The same piece of pottery he had just abracadabra-ed away. Chance seemed to recognize that this stranger was part of the trick. She squirmed in Colin's arms and cackled with baby laughter.

The man looked Colin right in the eyes. "I promise I'll make very good time," he repeated. "I'm the most reliable driver in all of Britain. Not one fare ever arrived late." He grinned again with obvious pride and stood up rather straighter. Then carefully, he handed the piece of pottery to Colin.

"Who the hell are you?" Colin asked.

194

TWENTY

As Emma sponged his face, Brodie mumbled, "I shouldna kissed ye."

"Regretting it already, eh?" she said teasingly, although she knew what he meant.

"The fever ..."

"Will break," she said resolutely.

"But it's our last ..."

"No, no it isn't. Don't think like that. This isn't the last play. The town will find a way to keep the tradition going, even without Destiny's money."

He shook his head, licked his chapped lips. "I meant it's our last day together."

Emma stood up from the sofa, stunned, and dropped the cloth back into the cold water. Things had been so busy and confusing that somehow she had managed to avoid facing this very obvious fact. Tomorrow was the first day of January, a new year. The day she was scheduled to depart Scotland. Tomorrow at this time she would be boarding her plane. She would be headed back to Providence and her classroom.

The door opened and Aileen walked in. "You don't have to worry, chickens," she said. "We have found a solution."

"Solution?" Emma asked. Brodie weakly struggled to prop himself up on an elbow and look towards his mother.

"To the riddle of Tommy, of course, and who is going to play him," said Aileen, pulling off her gloves and moving to put the kettle on the stove. "Joe is going to do it."

"I must be hallucinating," Brodie muttered.

"Joe?" Emma said. "Joe the Wish ..." She caught herself just in time. Even with all the strange things that had been happening, she would never be able to make Aileen and Brodie understand the Wish Granters. She wasn't even sure *she* understood them.

"Does he have any experience on the stage?" Brodie asked. "Can he sing or dance?"

"He knows the words, somehow," Aileen said. "Says he absorbed them just from a few days as a stagehand, can you imagine that? He must be one of those savant people with the wonderful memories like they show on the telly. The dancing can be worked around somehow. There's never a time when either the group of men or Emma isn't on the stage with him—and you can lead them through, can't you, love?" Aileen spooned tea leaves into her pot and looked at them levelly. "Not ideal, we all know that. But what else is there to do? Half our audience is already in town, checking into their rooms."

"There's nothing else that can be done," Emma agreed, praying that there was some variation of Wish Granter magic that would somehow carry Joe through. To continue to talk about it would just further upset Brodie, who had fallen back to the sofa with a thump. "But the singing ..."

"Ah, yes, thank you for nudging my memory." Aileen rummaged through one of the lower kitchen drawers, pulling out maps, trivets, scissors, scraps of paper, a pot holder, until she finally fished out a cassette tape. "He's just going to move his lips like the pop singers do on tour while Colin's voice comes out of the machine."

196

"Oh Lord," Brodie moaned.

"He's American, isn't he? The audience will love it to be sure. Now let me find those programs," Aileen muttered. "We had to mark out Colin's name and add Brodie's and now we'll have to mark that out and put Joe's. What did you say his last name was, Emma? De Wish, something like that? How do you spell it?"

Colin awoke with a jolt, as if from a nightmare, disoriented and slightly dazed. Both he and little Chance were fast asleep before the cab was even out of London. It wasn't strange that she would take a nap, but with his own mind spinning with questions and doubts, Colin never would have guessed he'd succumb so easily. But there it was. He slept as much like a baby as Chance—a deep, dreamless sort of trancelike sleep that lulled his mind until he finally awakened with a sense of disorientation the way one sometimes does in a strange hotel after a tiring trip.

He had the sense he had slept for some time. Moving slowly, so as not to rouse his daughter, who was still drowsing on his lap, Colin snuck a look at his watch. 11:30. He eased Chance to the seat beside him, and covered her with his sweater, then slid up to the window separating him from his driver.

"Excuse me," he said, pushing aside the partition. "Where are we?"

"Just passed into Scotland."

Scotland? It wasn't possible. The cabbie had promised good time, but they had covered four hundred miles in two hours.

"What time is it?" he asked.

The cabbie squinted at his dash. He seemed older now than he had in London, and Colin thought for an old guy he was certainly a speed demon. And he had a bemused expression across his freckled cheeks. Colin could see that when the man looked in the rear-view mirror.

"11:32," the cabbie said. "Will you be wanting to stop for lunch when the little girl awakens?"

"I don't know what's going on here or how we could have gotten so far," Colin said in a low voice full of suspicion. Had he been drugged? Were they being kidnapped? Something was completely awry. "Who sent you, anyway? Who told you I needed to go to Scotland?"

"A friend. One who has your best interests at heart."

"Indeed. And does this friend have a name?"

"Perhaps you should rest while you can, Sir, if you don't mind the suggestion," the cabbie said. "You have your big performance tonight, and I imagine there will be quite a crowd."

"How do you know about my big performance? Who are you and how are we moving so fast?"

"A nap always makes a trip go faster. So if you'd like to lie back and ..."

"I don't want to lie back," Colin snapped, although strangely enough he was still sleepy. Something was definitely wrong. He'd slept all morning and felt like sleeping all afternoon as well. He had definitely been drugged. He looked down at Chance in panic. Was she sleeping too deeply? Was she in danger?

The cabbie noted his fear. "Sir?" he said.

"What?"

"The friend who sent me," the man said. "It was a young lady by the name of Skye McFae."

Emma left Brodie thrashing in a restless sleep while Aileen dutifully inked out Brodie's name on each program and printed "Joe DeWish" beneath it. When Emma arrived at the school, she learned that Dunn had already walked Joe through the blocking, including the dances, and that he had picked up the movements with the same admirable speed he had shown while learning the lines. But Joe was obviously terrified—walking and talking like a robot. He managed to lift Emma for the ballet, but it looked more like Tommy was loading bales of hay than dancing with a woman he loved.

"Take it easy," Emma whispered in his ear.

"I'm trying," Joe whispered. "But I swear this is the scariest thing I've ever tried to do in my life." Dying was easier, he thought, and he struggled again and again to relax and go with the dance. Why couldn't they be putting on a football musical? Now that would be more his speed.

The singing was the biggest test. They knew it would be. Dunn simply eliminated Tommy's solos in the group numbers, letting the entire chorus sing those lines. But there was no way around "Almost Like Being in Love" or the ditty Tommy sings as he's first approaching Brigadoon at the very beginning of the play. For that, they would need Colin—or at least the ghost of Colin's voice.

A couple of the local lads rigged the cassette player to the sound system—an aging, shaky beast literally held together with duct tape and baling wire. There was no way to disguise the magnified "click" of the audio tape coming on and thus alerting the audience to their last-minute trick. But even if Alloway had possessed the best sound system in the world, the expression of sheer terror on Joe's face when he attempted to sing would have given him up. They went through the opening song three times, with Dunn begging Joe to relax between each try.

"I'm sorry," Joe said to Emma, after one of the tries.

"You're getting better," she said. "Maybe if you looked at the audience while you sang instead of your feet ..."

"I don't mean that," Joe said. "Alanna and I failed you. After everything, it doesn't look like we're going to be able to grant your wish."

Emma shrugged. "That's small potatoes in the light of all that's happened. In fact, I don't even exactly remember what I wished for."

"You wanted to kiss Colin. You said you wanted to see him, but Alanna and I knew you really wanted to kiss him."

Emma laughed. "Oh that. Well, I got something much better, so don't worry about it."

"But doing the play opposite a clunker like me. I'm pretty sure that's not part of anybody's wish."

"I swear, you're getting better. Besides ..."

"I know, I know," Joe said with a sigh. "I'm all they've got."

TWENTY-ONE

At seven that evening, Alanna dispatched a group of the hardier men of Alloway, some of them already dressed in their kilts, to bring Skye and Brodie to the auditorium.

Skye, beautifully dressed in blue velvet, was carried in like a queen, her cast swathed in a pale green scarf. Brodie—whose fever had broken but who was still weak and, they cautioned, possibly contagious—was quarantined high above the crowd in the lighting booth. It was a rather grand term for a stage with only three lights and three settings. On, off, dim.

This year, Adam, the quiet farmer who had run the lights for as long as Brodie could remember, had an additional task. It was also his job to turn on the recorder for the two songs Joe would be lip-syncing. The addition of sound seemed to flummox Adam, so Brodie agreed to sit beside the cassette player and cue the music. It was hot up in the booth, so Brodie had taken off his jacket and scarf as he peered at the stage. This much at least was the same. It was set just as it had been in years past, and there was a decent crowd as well.

But looking down from this unique angle, it was like Brodie could see the production for the first time. It was homespun, to be sure: actors in costume doubling as ushers, children selling little homemade cakes in the lobby, Mrs. Alders banging away on the not-quite-perfectly-tuned piano. But it wasn't just the same people on stage every year; it was also the same people in the audience. Brodie could recognize half of them on sight and it was clear that New Year's Eve at *Brigadoon* was a tradition for these people as well, that they not only accepted but embraced the simplicity of the play. They sat munching cupcakes and holding their marked-up programs, some of them singing the score along with Mrs. Alders.

A forgiving crowd, to be sure, but whether or not they would forgive the theatrical atrocity which was about to be unleashed on them was at this point unknowable. Brodie had seen Joe on his way in and the man was so nervous he had already sweated straight through his Tufts T-shirt. He was standing alone, off to the side, pacing and muttering what Brodie could only hope were lines from the play. If that wasn't the case, good, solid, Joe had surely become unhinged from the pressure of appearing on stage. It was said stage fright could kill. Brodie hoped that wasn't the case tonight. And Emma. What about Emma? His thoughts were mainly of her and what would inevitably happen when she finally did get to see Colin. The storm keeping him away couldn't last forever. Emma would go back to London, and Colin would have heard about how she'd saved the play, so he would want to thank her in person. Such thoughts led down roads Brodie knew he should not travel, but he could not prevent the thoughts from dogging him. So he watched the stage and the audience and tried hard to keep his mind on the task in front of him.

"I can't believe how calm you are," Alanna said to Emma.

"I'm actually excited," Emma said.

"You'll keep Joe on track?"

"He's going to be fine," Emma said. "It makes no sense, I know, but all day I've had the feeling this is going to turn out beautifully. You know that feeling? That despite appearances on the surface, everything is all right in the world?"

"Can't say that I do," said Alanna.

Emma laughed and hugged her, then darted off.

She's loving every minute of this, Alanna thought. This backstage world energizes her. She wondered if it had yet occurred to Emma that the romance she thought was missing in her life hadn't come from Colin but from the theater itself. Whatever happened between her and the various MacGregor lads, Emma needed to find a way to connect to the theater.

Joe was now hopping from one foot to another and, with a sigh, Alanna waved him over.

"At least try not to look so terrified," she said to him. "They aren't expecting you to be some great stage actor. They just need you to sell it."

"I know, I know," Joe said. "But do you know what's bugging me? Besides the fact I can't dance or sing or act, that is?"

"What?"

"Morgan isn't here."

"He isn't, is he?" Somehow in all the crush, Alanna had forgotten to look for him. Now that she thought of it, she hadn't seen him since Destiny had come to town. Destiny couldn't do something to Morgan, could she? Alanna wasn't exactly sure of the pecking order of power in Transition, but she had always assumed that Morgan ranked fairly high and was certainly not the sort of spirit who could be dispatched by a witch masquerading as a

London solicitor. But what if Destiny had much more power than she and Joe realized? It was strange indeed that Morgan had been MIA all day.

Of course, this was hardly the best time to tell Joe what she was thinking. He didn't need to speculate on the possibility Morgan was locked in some sort of supernatural battle between good and evil. He was worried enough about his ballet steps.

"Wake up," Morgan said. "We're here."

Colin's eyes slowly opened. How long had he slept this time? The sky outside the car window was very dark. But as he pushed himself to a sitting position and peered out, he could see the bridge of Alloway in the distance, lit with a hundred luminarias to mark the way. Beside him, little Chance was beginning to stir, and the clock on the dashboard said 7:54.

"I don't know who you are or how you did this," Colin said, "but you made a miracle this day. And I thank you for that."

"All just part of the job, sir."

"For you, Miss," said Townsperson Number Seven.

"Roses? They're beautiful, but where did they come from?" Emma reached out to take the huge spray of flowers with a perplexed look. There weren't any florists in Alloway.

"Kids found them in the lobby," the man said. "But your name's on the envelope."

Frowning, Emma fumbled for the small white envelope and pulled out the card.

Break a leg
Destiny Bane

Very funny, Emma thought, dropping the flowers to the nearest chair. And wasn't it odd that the standard good-luck wish of the theater could sound so much like a curse, Emma thought. But why would Destiny send her flowers?

It was obvious from the cold way Brodie had greeted his cousin's wife that the village had no love for Destiny, but Emma wondered: Was the woman really evil? She looked back down at the note in her hand. "Break a leg." Skye actually had and, for the first time, Emma felt a vague sense of something being off-kilter. That fall—the event that had changed the course of years of tradition, the fall that Emma assumed she had set in motion. For an instant she wondered if that fall had really been her fault or if some other influence had been at work. Thoughts can sometimes fly by so fast, they hardly register; and such thoughts—the ones that have no weight at all—can be dismissed as easily as swatting at a moth that flits away to safety. So Emma's thought evaporated. She had so much to do. So much to concentrate on. So many depending on her for the next few hours. She had to stay in the moment.

Colin burst through the back door of the auditorium with the force of the storm he'd left in London. He plunked Chance into the arms of his startled Aunt Aileen and rushed to the dressing room without stopping to say a word.

"I'm going to faint," Joe said. "Or maybe puke."

"I'll be in the first row," Alanna said. "Just keep saying the lines to me. Pretend I'm the only one out there." She sounded so certain, but her heart pounding away like a kettle drum told a different tale. She smiled bravely at Joe and mouthed, "I'm proud of you," before she walked unsteadily to take her seat down front.

Brodie squinted down into the auditorium. The musical prelude was winding down, the house lights had been lowered, and they were almost ready to begin. But suddenly he saw his mother come sprinting out a side door with baby Chance in her arms and saw her carry the child to where Skye was sitting.

If little Chance was here, that must mean Colin was here. Brodie sat with his finger poised above the tape recorder, unsure what to do next. This whole night had turned into a contradiction, but one thought came back

206

to Brodie now—and that thought was about Emma and his cousin Colin.

The lights rose to reveal the set—a set that was clearly based on the very town the audience had driven through on their way to see the play. They approved and applauded with enthusiasm. There was an air of happy expectation in the room, a room filled with people who wanted to believe the unbelievable, if just for a brief time.

Emma stood downstage left, waiting for the first notes of music. She closed her eyes, said a quick prayer, took a deep breath.

Joe, waiting downstage right, tense and taut, jumped when Aileen came up behind him and stood on tiptoe to whisper in his ear.

The music began, and Emma stepped from the wings. The scene where Fiona first sees Tommy was not only the first scene but one of her favorites. She turned toward the side of the stage where Joe would be emerging and prepared to act startled.

In fact, her surprise was not an act.

TWENTY-TWO

When Colin MacGregor entered downstage right in full costume, the room erupted in applause. This was the man they had traveled to see. Over the years, his reputation had grown. A few local papers had even done pieces about his performances and his burgeoning career in London. Now here he was in person.

Emma, her arms full of flowers, turned. But instead of finding Joe, as she'd expected, there was Colin.

Colin also turned. But instead of finding Skye he faced Emma.

Certainly recognizable since the last time he'd seen her, still it took him a second to process the shock. For a moment he was sixteen again and back in America where he and Emma had played these roles before. Emma's face lit up with real surprise and then, as recognition seeped in, she felt confused and off-kilter. Expecting to turn and see Joe as her leading man, she had prepared herself mentally, but now there was Colin. Everything she'd wished for was coming true. But what should she do about it? She felt drawn back in time to their high school production and wondered what year this was and where they were.

She had thought about this moment so often, wondered if he would look the same, act the same, be the same Colin as before. And what about her? Would he still find her alluring, still be drawn to her? So many years had passed. Was anything left of what might have been?

All the turmoil to get to this point faded away as they began the opening song. And isn't that the way with theatrical productions? Turmoil and chaos, and then—if cast and crew have done their parts—a performance takes place that seems to have a life of its own. So Emma as Fiona and Colin as Tommy walked toward each other and began to sing. It was as if there had never been any years between them.

Colin was the more polished. The years of classes and coaching had turned him from a stage-struck boy into an actor.

In the first row, Alanna couldn't contain her relief as Morgan slid into the next seat.

"It's a miracle," she whispered.

"This was rather a challenge, wasn't it?" he answered.

Alanna's relief seemed to run through the whole auditorium. Backstage, Joe leaned against a wall, weak and rattled. Aileen and Dunn stood beaming beside him.

"'Tis a miracle that Colin made it here," Dunn whispered.

The other actors rallied in spirit. The play was going to be a great success; that was clear before Emma and Colin had finished the first verse of their song. All the residents of Alloway heaved a collective sigh of relief and settled in happily to enjoy their big night.

But there were two people in the crowded school room who felt a mix of emotions. The incomprehensible arrival of Colin in the midst of the snowstorm meant the play would be a success. Important, of course, but ...

For Brodie and Skye, Colin's arrival might mean the end of other wishes. Surely wishing wasn't limited to Emma on this night. In a way, everyone comes to a play with some wish, even if it's only to suspend real life for a little while and forget the troublesome world. Brodie and Skye sat in silence with Colin and Emma up on stage as the reunion happened in real time but not in real life.

"Is she a better Fiona than me?" Skye wondered and then was immediately ashamed of the thought. She pulled Colin's daughter more closely to her, rocking the child back and forth despite the pain it caused her leg. What she had prayed for had happened. Colin was back. So why was her heart heavy as she waited in the dark, as she counted down the scenes to their kiss?

Above her, in the lighting booth, Brodie was in even more agony. Emma had accepted him as the stand-in gracefully enough, had kissed him and seemed to care. But now the real article was back in town. Colin was taller and more gallant, with a lighter step and a deeper voice. The man she'd come so far to see was here before her, and who could blame Emma if she got swept up in the romance of it all? No woman had ever been drawn to Brodie while Colin MacGregor was in the room, and perhaps tonight would be no different. And, Brodie assumed, Colin had changed over these years—become more worldly, gotten used to the attention of women while he, Brodie, was still a farmer, toiling in the fields with no adoring fans save the sheep and chickens.

The play progressed, scene after scene. At ten minutes to midnight, Dunn gave Joe the signal and he slipped out of the back door, ran across the lawn and up the steps to the bell tower of the church. This time he remembered the foam earmuffs. He clapped them over his ears and stood for a few minutes, panting and waiting for the signal. And when it came, he threw all his weight into ringing the bell.

Midnight. One year slipping into another. The passing of time, Joe thought, and even though time no longer meant the same thing to him, he knew he and Alanna must still pause for a moment, to acknowledge this night where the world seems to pause. Only sixty seconds to pause and to hover, looking both backward and forward.

On stage, with the sound of the first bell, Emma closed her eyes. Colin put a hand on each of her arms, bent towards her. She exhaled slightly, tilting her chin.

And then she got her wish. Colin's lips were warm and soft, slightly parted. His touch was firm without being rough. It felt like memory and youth and excitement and glamour and hope. It was as she had remembered it. Colin's kiss held the same magic.

Emma was smiling as they pulled away and the last church bell rang. She felt a great sense of completion, of something in her life coming full circle. The spell of Colin MacGregor was officially broken. The same man who had carried her into the fantasy had carried her out.

"How did you get here?" Colin whispered.

"Magic," she whispered back.

"Aye," he said. "That's how I traveled as well."

They joined hands and turned toward the audience as the lights slowly rose on the stage. Emma squinted toward the large bright light in the center and the small room where Brodie was waiting. She moved her lips very slightly, so slightly that, watching her from so far away, Brodie wondered if he had dreamed the message.

"I love you too," he said back.

"What?" asked Adam, standing beside him.

"Nothing," Brodie answered quickly. "Pull up the house light."

It was a new year. It began a new life.

As the bells of midnight rang, Destiny stood on her terrace, gazing down at the celebrating crowd in the street below. A cashmere shawl was thrown over her shoulders, a glass of champagne in her hand.

The Wish Granters may have taken the first round, but she was not distressed. Her withdrawal had been voluntary. She had even been gracious in the moment of loss. She had sent roses, had she not?

In fact, letting Alanna and Joe off easy this time was part of her overall plan. When playing chess—another game Destiny enjoyed—she would often allow her opponent to take a few early pawns as a way of lulling him into a false sense of security. Let Alanna and Joe believe they had beaten her in Alloway. It only meant that the next time they met, when she unleashed more of her power, they would be stunned and unprepared for her strength.

Destiny took another sip of champagne and smiled. New Year's was her favorite holiday. All those innocents down below her—in London and across the world—would shortly be making New Year's resolutions. They would want to lose weight, pay off their credit cards, manage their tempers, or learn to speak French. All those fragile little newborn wishes, so easy to crush. By the end of the month, she would have defeated most of them, and each small failure would make it just a little harder to wish the next time.

A wish-free universe—this was Destiny's goal. A world where people could be manipulated into anything. A world where people had no hope in the future and no faith in the power of a wish.

TWENTY-THREE

The play had been a success, but Brodie was not happy. "I canna believe this is goodbye," he said. "It's like I just found you and already the fates have conspired to take you away."

"It's only goodbye for a short time," Emma reassured him. "I have to finish out the school year, but then I promise I'll be back." And she would be. Back to Brodie. Back to Alloway and the school that needed a drama teacher, the town that needed someone to publicize *Brigadoon* throughout Britain. She could see her future—all of it—stretching out before her like pages in a book.

But Brodie's face was still doubtful. "You'll get back home to America," he said, "and it may not be so easy. You'll remember all the things you'd be giving up. Your fine restaurants and shops, your streaming TV, your Wi-Fi."

Emma laughed softly and buried her face in his neck. "That's what you think will tempt me? Fancy restaurants and Wi-Fi that surely we can get here? You must believe me when I tell you that everything I've ever wanted is right here." She slid her arms farther around his neck until her mouth was just at his ear. "Everything."

It was the morning after the play: January the first—a new day and a new year. The day when the holiday season ends and the world begins to reluctantly turn back to the business of everyday life. The audience had spent the night in the various homes of Alloway, had risen to eat their breakfasts—often dining across the table from members of the cast. Rather than a sequence of cabs,

Morgan had arranged for a charter bus to take them all back to Edinburgh and then points beyond. The bus sat steaming and trembling on the far side of the bridge. Yes, it was a time for goodbyes but also a time for reflecting and looking ahead. Brodie still could not believe that this lovely lass had chosen him. Emma felt, for the first time in many years, the completeness of real love. Not that fantasy thing she'd been carrying around on her shoulders, but something that would last and grow, something with permanence and roots. She would be surrounded by this loving family, take part in their joys and sorrows, watch the planting season arrive and the sowing season end. See the sheep in the meadows and the goats on the hills. And every year, Alloway would host their little production to an audience hungry for a magic respite from the everyday of their lives.

"Thank you for everything," Alanna said. She hugged Aunt Aileen, surprised at feeling a little choked up. It came with the territory of being a Wish Granter, she supposed—a constant stream of hellos and goodbyes. But she wasn't sure she'd ever get used to all this leaving. Alanna stepped back and sighed, let her vision drift once more over every detail of the village.

As if reading her mind, Aileen said, "You're always welcome here, love. You can come back whenever you wish, and here we'll be, just the same."

Alanna nodded, not completely trusting her voice to speak. She blew a kiss to Skye, who stood in her doorway, little Chance balanced on her hip, and shot a smile at Colin, who was in the shadows behind them, his hand lightly resting on Skye's shoulder. They wrote the ending of their story on their own, she thought. They would be a family.

"You know," Aileen was saying to Joe. "I've had time to consider it all, and I think you're a bit of a softie."

Joe snorted a little in indignation, to cover up the fact he was damn close to crying himself. "Nah, I'm all business, Aileen; you know that."

She pursed her lips. "Maybe so," she said, "but exactly what is your business? I still can't figure that. Well, never mind," she added, throwing her arms wide and inviting Joe in for a hug. "You'll always have a home here too, if you wanna, if you need a place to settle when your wandering days are through, Mr. Joe DeWish."

Joe nodded, while he hugged her awkwardly and slapped her on the shoulder as if she were a guy. Would he ever need a place to settle? Ever since the morning his car had been crushed and he had become a Wish Granter, he'd been obsessed with one thought: that he must get back to Earth and avenge his death. And that of his partner, Russ, as well. That he must unearth every clue and find every answer, thinking that nothing but the truth would set him free. That nothing but revenge would complete his story. But now, gazing into Aileen's kindly old eyes, he wondered if that were really true.

"I'll see you again," he said. He wasn't sure when or how, but he felt sure it would happen.

Across the cobblestone courtyard, Dunn held out a hand to Morgan. "I shall miss you most of all," he said. "You were by far the best cab driver that Alloway has ever had."

Morgan roared with laughter, then pulled a whistle out of his pocket. A couple of short blasts and he had the attention of everyone in the courtyard. "The bus pulls out in two minutes," he said. "We need to start moving."

The stragglers in the crowd began to head across the bridge. While Brodie was bidding goodbye to Joe and Alanna, Colin appeared briefly by Emma's side.

"You came all this way," he said. "And we never really had the chance to talk. What brought you to Alloway, after all this time?"

"You," Emma said honestly. "Or rather the memory of you. I came to Alloway for one reason, and one reason alone. I came to kiss you."

Colin's brow wrinkled a little, the beginning of a frown.

"But that's over," Emma hastened to add. "I'd told myself for years that you were the one that got away. You know that phrase? We Americans say it. There's always the idea of that one ideal person, that perfect match or fit or soul mate, whatever you choose to call it. And for years I told myself that my ideal person was you. But I see now that you weren't my destination. You were the road that would lead me there. I finally feel part of a loving family. A family that needs me as much as I need them. I fell in love with Alloway and its people and Brodie, all while you were just a cloud in my memory."

Colin nodded. "I feel your coming here has done the same thing for me, although I can't say exactly how. But with you and Brodie ..."

Emma knew where he was headed and cut him off with a laugh. "Don't worry. I'm not some dopey girl who thinks she falls in love each time she plays opposite a boy in a play. This isn't some schoolgirl fling for me, and I don't intend to break your cousin's heart. I hope this doesn't sound rude or dismissive, but you and Brodie are completely different to me. You were always the fantasy. And Brodie is real."

"That he is," Colin agreed, grinning in relief. "As real as rock."

Morgan gave another whistle blast. "Last call," he yelled.

"This must all be a tremendous relief to you," Alanna said to Joe. "Emma did kiss Colin. So I guess we get credit for this case after all."

"Thank God for that at least," Joe said. "I was beginning to think I'd frozen my ass off here in MacHootersville for nothing."

"You know," Alanna said, "Everyone in MacHootersville found out that you're a nice guy."

Joe raised a finger to his lips. "Hush," he said. "The humans will hear you."

Emma clung to Brodie. "You better come to the States in March like you promised," she told him.

"And you better be back here in June," he said.

She nodded, kissed him again, and then turned to find Joe and Alanna waiting for her.

"Come on, Emma," Joe said. "No need to walk alone."

She nodded bravely and took Joe's arm on one side, Alanna's on the other. Without them practically dragging her across the bridge, she wasn't sure she would have had the strength to make it. As her foot left the last cobblestone of the bridge, Emma stopped.

"I've just had the most awful thought," she said. "What if none of this was real? What if the three of us have been in the true Brigadoon and, when we turn around, there will be nothing there? Everyone will have faded into the mist for a hundred years."

The three of them stood for a moment, immobile. The bus waiting in front of them, the bridge behind.

"Only one way to find out," Joe said. "On three we all turn and look. One ... two ... three ..."

And then Emma felt herself being spun around, with Brodie's strong arms wrapped around her. He'd run across the bridge for one final kiss, and they were so swept up in each other and the moment that neither of them had been conscious of the bus or the bridge, the time or the place. They didn't even notice that Joe and Alanna were no longer there. And no one in Alloway, not Emma or Brodie or Aunt Aileen or Skye or Dunn, not Colin and not little Chance would ever remember they'd been there at all.

"Well, that was a pretty dramatic exit, if I say so myself," Alanna whispered. They were being pulled from the scene as if through a crystal tube, the snow-covered hills beneath them growing ever smaller and less distinct. "Good job."

"I had nothing to do with it," Joe said. "Which only leaves ..."

And they were aware Morgan was with them, also rocketing through space and time.

"Wait a minute," said Alanna. "Who's driving that bus?"

"You think I can manifest a whole bus and I can't provide the driver?" Morgan said with a laugh. "Well, I certainly hope you two enjoyed your little holiday in Scotland, where your only problem was trying to decide which of those nice people was the nicest. But I have to warn you that the next case will be a little tougher."

Joe reached for Alanna's hand. She grabbed it and held on tight. They hurtled at high speed now and, if being a Wish Granter had taught her anything, it was that some transitions were bumpier than others.

"Where are we headed?" she called out to Morgan, hoping he could hear her above the whipping wind.

"To a place," Morgan said, "where a woman is using all her wiles to get out of a very dicey situation and a decision she made a whole year ago. It seemed a good idea at the time, but things got complicated for her. At the time she thought the future would take care of itself, but she found out that the future arrives before you expect it and brings with it circumstances you couldn't foresee. We're headed to the land of opportunity, and to a crime scene. To a place, come to think of it, that is the quite the opposite of Alloway. A place called Boston."

About The Author

L B Gschwandtner is the multiple award-winning author of eight books under her own name and two books under her pen name, Bea Alexander. Her novel, *The Other New Girl*, was a USA Best Book Awards winner and received an honorable mention from Reader Views Literary Awards. You can see all her books at lbgschwandtner.com.

Website: Lbgschwandtner.com
Bluesky: @lbgwriter.bsky.social
Facebook: www.facebook.com/LBGschwandtner
& Bea Alexander Author
https://www.facebook.com/profile.php?id=61571339319956

Books by L B Gschwandtner

The Other New Girl (Teenagers in trouble at a Quaker boarding school)
The Wish Granters series: They'll grant a woman one wish; the rest is up to her.
Shelly's Second Chance (The Wish Granters, Book One)
Carla's Secret (The Wish Granters, Book Two)
Emma's New Love (The Wish Granters, Book Three)

The Naked Gardener (a woman gardens naked then goes on a wild canoe trip with gal pals)

Page Truly and The Journey To Nearandfar (a fantasy for middle graders who love adventure and imagining what might be)

<u>Maybelle's Revenge</u> (short stories with a twist)

<u>Foxy's Tale</u> (mother/daughter angst with an incompetent vampire)
Coauthored with Karen Cantwell

Books by Bea Alexander (pen name)

Recipe for a Witch (YA witchy story about what happens when 18-year-old Amanda discovers she has spellcasting powers)

Escape to Zendara (dystopian love story with multiple plot twists set against the backdrop of a corrupt city)

All available at Amazon.com or order from your local bookseller.

For those who would like to read the entire poem, "Tam O'Shanter" (in English)

By Robert Burns

When the peddler people leave the streets,
And thirsty neighbours, neighbours meet;
As market days are wearing late,
And folk begin to take the road home,
While we sit boozing strong ale,
And getting drunk and very happy,
We don't think of the long Scots miles,
The marshes, waters, steps and stiles,
That lie between us and our home,
Where sits our sulky, sullen dame (wife),
Gathering her brows like a gathering storm,
Nursing her wrath, to keep it warm.

This truth finds honest Tam o' Shanter,
As he from Ayr one night did canter;
Old Ayr, which never a town surpasses,
For honest men and bonny lasses.

Oh Tam, had you but been so wise,
As to have taken your own wife Kate's advice!
She told you well you were a waster,
A rambling, blustering, drunken boaster,
That from November until October,
Each market day you were not sober;
During each milling period with the miller,
You sat as long as you had money,
For every horse he put a shoe on,
The blacksmith and you got roaring drunk on;
That at the Lords House, even on Sunday,
You drank with Kirkton Jean till Monday.
She prophesied, that, late or soon,
You would be found deep drowned in Doon,
Or caught by warlocks in the murk,
By Alloway's old haunted church.

Ah, gentle ladies, it makes me cry,
To think how many counsels sweet,
How much long and wise advice
The husband from the wife despises!

But to our tale: One market night,
Tam was seated just right,
Next to a fireplace, blazing finely,
With creamy ales, that drank divinely;
And at his elbow, Cobbler Johnny,
His ancient, trusted, thirsty crony;
Tom loved him like a very brother,
They had been drunk for weeks together.
The night drove on with songs and clatter,
And every ale was tasting better;
The landlady and Tam grew gracious,
With secret favours, sweet and precious;
The cobbler told his queerest stories;
The landlord's laugh was ready chorus:
Outside, the storm might roar and rustle,
Tam did not mind the storm a whistle.

Care, mad to see a man so happy,
Even drowned himself in ale.
As bees fly home with loads of treasure,
The minutes winged their way with pleasure:
Kings may be blessed, but Tam was glorious,
Over all the ills of life victorious.

But pleasures are like poppies spread:
You seize the flower, its bloom is shed;
Or like the snow fall on the river,
A moment white—then melts forever,
Or like the Aurora Borealis rays,
That move before you can point to their place;
Or like the rainbow's lovely form,
Vanishing amid the storm.
No man can tether time or tide,
The hour approaches Tom must ride:
That hour, of night's black arch—the key-stone,
That dreary hour he mounts his beast in
And such a night he takes to the road in
As never a poor sinner had been out in.

    The wind blew as if it had blown its last;
The rattling showers rose on the blast;
The speedy gleams the darkness swallowed,
Loud, deep and long the thunder bellowed:
That night, a child might understand,
The Devil had business on his hand.

    Well mounted on his grey mare, Meg.
A better never lifted leg,
Tom, raced on through mud and mire,
Despising wind and rain and fire;
Whilst holding fast his good blue bonnet,
While crooning over some old Scots sonnet,
Whilst glowering round with prudent care,
Lest ghosts catch him unaware:
Alloway's Church was drawing near,
Where ghosts and owls nightly cry.

By this time he was across the ford,
Where in the snow the pedlar got smothered;
And past the birch trees and the huge stone,
Where drunken Charlie broke his neck bone;
And through the thorns, and past the monument,
Where hunters found the murdered child;
And near the thorn, above the well,
Where Mungo's mother hanged herself.
Before him the river Doon pours all his floods;
The doubling storm roars throught the woods;
The lightnings flashes from pole to pole;
Nearer and more near the thunder rolls;
When, glimmering through the groaning trees,
Alloway's Church seemed in a blaze,
Through every gap , light beams were glancing,
And loud resounded mirth and dancing.

Inspiring, bold John Barleycorn! (whisky)
What dangers you can make us scorn!
With ale, we fear no evil;
With whisky, we'll face the Devil!
The ales so swam in Tam's head,
Fair play, he didn't care a farthing for devils.
But Maggie stood, right sore astonished,
Till, by the heel and hand admonished,
She ventured forward on the light;
And, vow! Tom saw an incredible sight!

Warlocks and witches in a dance:
No cotillion, brand new from France,
But hornpipes, jigs, strathspeys, and reels,
Put life and mettle in their heels.
In a window alcove in the east,
There sat Old Nick, in shape of beast;
A shaggy dog, black, grim, and large,
To give them music was his charge:
He screwed the pipes and made them squeal,
Till roof and rafters all did ring.
Coffins stood round, like open presses,
That showed the dead in their last dresses;
And, by some devilish magic sleight,
Each in its cold hand held a light:
By which heroic Tom was able
To note upon the holy table,
A murderer's bones, in gibbet-irons;
Two span-long, small, unchristened babies;
A thief just cut from his hanging rope -
With his last gasp his mouth did gape;
Five tomahawks with blood red-rusted;
Five scimitars with murder crusted;
A garter with which a baby had strangled;
A knife a father's throat had mangled -
Whom his own son of life bereft -
The grey-hairs yet stack to the shaft;
With more o' horrible and awful,
Which even to name would be unlawful.
Three Lawyers' tongues, turned inside out,
Sown with lies like a beggar's cloth -
Three Priests' hearts, rotten, black as muck
Lay stinking, vile, in every nook.

As Thomas glowered, amazed, and curious,
The mirth and fun grew fast and furious;
The piper loud and louder blew,
The dancers quick and quicker flew,
They reeled, they set, they crossed, they linked,
Till every witch sweated and smelled,
And cast her ragged clothes to the floor,
And danced deftly at it in her underskirts!

Now Tam, O Tam! had these been young girls,
All plump and strapping in their teens!
Their underskirts, instead of greasy flannel,
Been snow-white seventeen hundred linen!
The trousers of mine, my only pair,
That once were plush, of good blue hair,
I would have given them off my buttocks
For one blink of those pretty girls!

But withered hags, old and droll,
Ugly enough to suckle a foal,
Leaping and flinging on a stick,
Its a wonder it didn't turn your stomach!

230

But Tam knew what was what well enough:
There was one winsome, jolly wench,
That night enlisted in the core,
Long after known on Carrick shore
(For many a beast to dead she shot,
And perished many a bonnie boat,
And shook both much corn and barley,
And kept the country-side in fear.)
Her short underskirt, o' Paisley cloth,
That while a young lass she had worn,
In longitude though very limited,
It was her best, and she was proud...
Ah! little knew your reverend grandmother,
That underskirt she bought for her little grandaughter,
With two Scots pounds (it was all her riches),
Would ever graced a dance of witches!

But here my tale must stoop and bow,
Such words are far beyond her power;
To sing how Nannie leaped and kicked
(A supple youth she was, and strong);
And how Tom stood like one bewitched,
And thought his very eyes enriched;
Even Satan glowered, and fidgeted full of lust,
And jerked and blew with might and main;
Till first one caper, then another,
Tom lost his reason all together,
And roars out: "Well done, short skirt!"
And in an instant all was dark;
And scarcely had he Maggie rallied,
When out the hellish legion sallied.

As bees buzz out with angry wrath,
When plundering herds assail their hive;
As a wild hare's mortal foes,
When, pop! she starts running before their nose;
As eager runs the market-crowd,
When "Catch the thief!" resounds aloud:
So Maggie runs, the witches follow,
With many an unearthly scream and holler.

     Ah, Tom! Ah, Tom! You will get what's coming!
In hell they will roast you like a herring!
In vain your Kate awaits your coming!
Kate soon will be a woeful woman!
Now, do your speedy utmost, Meg,
And beat them to the key-stone of the bridge;
There, you may toss your tale at them,
A running stream they dare not cross!
But before the key-stone she could make,
She had to shake a tail at the fiend;
For Nannie, far before the rest,
Hard upon noble Maggie pressed,
And flew at Tam with furious aim;
But little knew she Maggie's mettle!
One spring brought off her master whole,
But left behind her own grey tail:
The witch caught her by the rump,
And left poor Maggie scarce a stump.

     Now, who this tale of truth shall read,
Each man, and mother's son, take heed:
Whenever to drink you are inclined,
Or short skirts run in your mind,
Think! you may buy joys over dear:
Remember Tam o' Shanter's mare.